The Signors of the Night

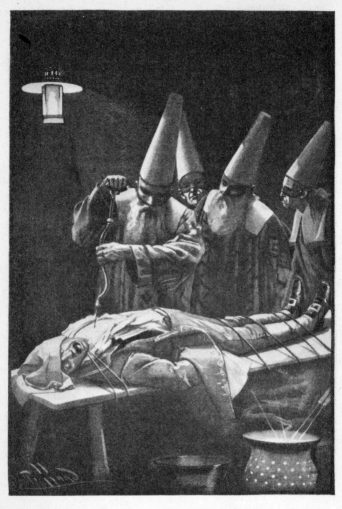

"HE UTTERED A LOW MOAN AS HE FELT THE SHINING STEEL
CUT HIS FLESH."

The
Signors of the Night

The Story of Frà Giovanni, the Soldier-
Monk of Venice; and of others
in the " Silent City"

By

Max Pemberton

"When Venice sate in state, throned on her hundred isles"
Byron

Short Story Index Reprint Series

BOOKS FOR LIBRARIES PRESS
FREEPORT, NEW YORK

First Published 1899
Reprinted 1970

INTERNATIONAL STANDARD BOOK NUMBER:
0-8369-3680-9

LIBRARY OF CONGRESS CATALOG CARD NUMBER:
74-132123

PRINTED IN THE UNITED STATES OF AMERICA

AUTHOR'S FOREWORD

I WOULD take this opportunity of saying that, in two instances at least, the central idea of these stories is to be found in the history of Venice in the more dramatic years of the seventeenth and eighteenth centuries. Few of those who remember Mr. Horatio F. Brown's delightful *Venetian Studies* will fail to recognise the alchemist Marcantonio Bragadino in my sketch of the charlatan Zuane de Franza. It is to be doubted if there is, in the whole story of chicanery, a more remarkable figure than that of Bragadino, whose ultimate exposure was in a measure due to the powerful sermons preached against him by Frà Paolo Sarpi. It has been my hope in these sketches to portray in Frà Giovanni, the Capuchin monk, something of that confliction of idea which permitted a priest to wield so great an influence in a

Republic which by no means loved priests. Nor do I think that the measure of authority here permitted to Frà Giovanni would have been denied to the great friar who won religious liberty for the Venetians.

For the story "A Miracle of Bells," the Spanish Conspiracy is my authority. It is curious that a church figured so often in the narratives of such plottings as these. The student will remember that a document hidden in a foldstool of the church of the Frari betrayed the Giambattista Bragadin to the police.

Elsewhere, for knowledge of the zanni of Venice, I am indebted to the widely-known memoirs of Count Carlo Gozzi.

MAX PEMBERTON.

LONDON, 1899.

CONTENTS

ILLUSTRATIONS

ILLUSTRATIONS

The Signors of the Night

THE RISEN DEAD

I

THE sun was setting on the second day of June, in the year 1701, when Pietro Falier, the Captain of the Police of Venice, quitted his office in the Piazzetta of St. Mark and set out, alone, for the Palace of Frà Giovanni, the Capuchin friar, who lived over on the Island of the Guidecca.

"I shall return in an hour," he said to his subordinate as he stepped into the black gondola which every Venetian knew so well. "If any has need of me, I am at the house of Frà Giovanni."

The subordinate saluted, and returned slowly toward the Ducal palace. He was thinking that his Captain went overmuch just then to the house of that strange friar who had come to Venice so mysteriously, and so mysteriously had won the favour of the republic.

"Saint John!" he muttered to himself, "that we should dance attendance on a shaven crown, — we, who were the masters of the city a year ago! What is the Captain thinking of? Are we all women, then, or have women plucked our brains that it should be Frà Giovanni this and Frà Giovanni that, and your tongue snapped off if you so much as put a question. To the devil with all friars, say I."

The good fellow stopped a moment in his walk to lay the flat of his sword across the shoulders of a mountebank, who had dared to remain seated at the door of his booth while so great a person passed. Then he returned to his office, and whispered in the ear of his colleague the assurance that the Captain was gone again to the island of the Jews, and that his business was with the friar.

"And look you, Michele," said he, "it is neither to you nor to me that he comes nowadays. Not a whisper of it, as I live, except to this friar, whom I could crush between my fingers as a glass ball out of Murano."

His colleague shook his head.

"There have been many," said he, "who have tried to crush Frà Giovanni. They grin between the bars of dungeons, my friend, —

at least, those who have heads left to grin with. Be warned of me, and make an ally of the man who has made an ally of Venice. The Captain knows well what he is doing. If he has gone to the priest's house now, it is that the priest may win rewards for us again, as he has won them already a hundred times."

He spoke earnestly, though, in truth, his guess was not a good one. The Captain of the Police had not gone to the Island of the Guidecca to ask a service of the friar; he had gone, as he thought, to save the friar's life. At the moment when his subordinates were wagging their heads together, he himself stood in the priest's house, before the very table at which Frà Giovanni sat busy with his papers and his books.

"I implore you to listen to me, Prince!" he had just exclaimed very earnestly, as he repeated the news for the second time, and stood clamorous for the answer to his question.

The friar, who was dressed in the simple habit of the Capuchins, and who wore his cowl over his head so that only his shining black eyes could be seen, put down his pen when he heard himself addressed as " Prince."

"Captain," he said sharply, "who is this person you come here to warn? You speak of him as 'Prince.' It is some other, then, and not myself?"

The Captain bit his lip. He was one of the four in Venice who knew something of Frà Giovanni's past.

"Your Excellency's pardon," he exclaimed very humbly; "were we not alone, you would find me more discreet. I know well that the Prince of Iseo is dead, — in Venice at least. But to Frà Giovanni, his near kinsman, I say beware, for there are those here who have sworn he shall not live to say Mass again."

For an instant a strange light came into the priest's eyes. But he gave no other sign either of surprise or of alarm.

"They have sworn it — you know their names, then, Captain?"

"The police do not concern themselves with names, Excellency."

"Which means that you do not know their names, Captain?"

Pietro Falier sighed. This friar never failed to humble him, he thought. If it were not for the honours which the monk had obtained for the police since he began his work in Venice, the Captain said that he would not lift a hand to save him from the meanest bravo in Italy.

"You do not know their names, Captain — confess, confess," continued the priest, raising his hand in a bantering gesture; "you come to me with some gossip of the bed-chamber, your ears have been open in the market-place, and this tittle-tattle is your purchase — confess, confess."

The Captain flushed as he would have done before no other in all Venice.

"I do not know their names, Excellency," he stammered; "it is gossip from the *bravo's* kitchen. They say that you are to die before Mass to-morrow. I implore you not to leave this house to-night. We shall know how to do the rest if you will but remain indoors."

It was an earnest entreaty, but it fell upon deaf ears. The priest answered by taking a sheet of paper and beginning to write upon it.

"I am indebted to you, Signor Falier," said he, quietly, "and you know that I am not the man to forget my obligations. None the less, I fear that I must disregard your warning, for I have an appointment in the market to-night, and my word is not so easily broken. Let me reassure you a little. The news that you bring to me, and for which I am your debtor, was known to me three days ago. Here upon this paper I have written down the name of the woman and of her confederates who have hired the *bravo* Rocca to kill me to-night in the shadow of the church of San Salvatore. You will read that paper and the woman's name — when you have my permission."

Falier stepped back dumb with amazement.

"The woman's name, Excellency," he repeated, so soon as his surprise permitted him to speak, "you know her, then?"

"Certainly, or how could I write it upon the paper?"

"But you will give that paper to me, here and now. Think, Excellency, if she is your enemy, she is the enemy also of Venice. What forbids that we arrest her at once? You may not be alive at dawn!"

"In which case," exclaimed the priest, satirically, "the Signori of the Night would be well able to answer for the safety of the city. Is it not so, Captain?"

Falier stammered an excuse.

"We have not your eyes, Excellency; we cannot work miracles — but at least we can try to protect you from the hand of the

6

assassin. Name this woman to me, and she shall not live when midnight strikes."

Frà Giovanni rose from his chair and put his hand gently upon the other's shoulder.

"Signor Falier," said he, "if I told you this woman's name here and now as you ask, the feast of Corpus Christi might find a new Doge in Venice."

"You say, Excellency — ?"

"That the city is in danger as never she was before in her history."

"And your own life?"

"Shall be given for Venice if necessary. Listen to this : you seek to be of service to me. Have you any plan?"

"No plan but that which posts guards at your door and keeps you within these walls — "

"That the enemies of Venice may do their work. Is that your reason, Signor Falier?"

"I have no other reason, Excellency, but your own safety and that of the city."

"I am sure of it, Captain, and being sure I am putting my life in your hands to-night — "

"To-night; we are to follow you to the Merceria, then?"

"Not at all; say rather that you are to

return to the palace and to keep these things so secret that even the Council has no word of them.   But, at ten o'clock, take twenty of your best men and let your boat lie in the shadow of the church of San Luca until I have need of you.   You understand, Captain Falier?"

Falier nodded his head and replied vaguely. Truth to tell, he understood very little beyond this, — that the friar had been before him once more, and that he could but follow as a child trustingly.   And the city was in danger!   His heart beat quick when he heard the words.

"Excellency," he stammered, "the boat shall be there — at ten o'clock — in the shadow of the church of San Luca.   But first — "

"No," said the priest, quickly, "we have done with our firstly — and your gondola waits, I think, signorè!"

II

The bells of the Chapel of St. Mark were striking the hour of eight o'clock, when Frà Giovanni stepped from his gondola, and crossed the great square towards that laby-

rinth of narrow streets and winding alleys
they call the Merceria.

The Piazza itself was then ablaze with the
light of countless lamps; dainty lanterns,
coloured as the rainbow, swayed to the soft
breeze between the arches of the colonnade.
Nobles were seated at the doors of the
splendid cafés; the music of stringed instruments mingled with the louder, sweeter
music of the bells; women, whose jewels
were as sprays of flame, many-hued and
dazzling, hung timidly upon the arms of
lovers; gallants swaggered in costly velvets
and silks which were the spoil of the generous East; even cassocked priests and monks
in their sombre habits passed to and fro
amidst that glittering throng, come out to
herald the glory of a summer's night.

And clear and round, lifting themselves
up through the blue haze to the silent world
of stars above, were the domes and cupolas
of the great chapel itself, — the chapel which,
through seven centuries, had been the city's
witness to the God who had made her great,
and who would uphold her still before the
nations.

The priest passed through the crowd
swiftly, seeming to look neither to the right

nor to the left. The brown habit of the
Capuchins was his dress, and his cowl was
drawn so well over his head that only his
eyes were visible, — those eyes which stand
out so strangely in the many portraits which
are still the proud possession of Venice.
Though he knew well that an assassin waited
for him in the purlieus of the church of San
Salvatore, his step was quick and brisk; he
walked as a man who goes willingly to a
rendezvous, and anticipates its climax with
pleasure. When he had left the great square
with its blaze of lanterns and its babel of
tongues, and had begun to thread the narrow streets by which he would reach the
bridge of the Rialto, a smile played for a
moment about his determined mouth, and
he drew his capuce still closer over his ears.

" So it is Rocca whom they send, — Rocca,
the poltroon ! Surely there is the hand of
God in this."

He raised his eyes for a moment to the
starlit heaven, and then continued his brisk
walk. His way lay through winding alleys ;
over bridges so narrow that two men could
not pass abreast ; through passages where
rogues lurked, and repulsive faces were
thrust grinning into his own. But he knew

the city as one who had lived there all his life; and for the others, the thieves and scum of Venice, he had no thought. Not until he came out before the church of Santa Maria Formosa did he once halt or look behind him. The mystery of the night was a joy to him. Even in the shadow of the church, his rest was but for a moment; and, as he rested, the meaning smile hovered again upon his wan face.

" The play begins," he muttered, while he loosened slightly the girdle of his habit and thrust his right hand inside it; "the God of Venice give me courage."

A man was following him now, — he was sure of it. He had seen him as he turned to cross the bridge which would set him on the way to the church of San Salvatore, — a short, squat man, masked and dressed from head to foot in black. Quick as the movements of the fellow were, dexterous his dives into porches and the patches of shadow which the eaves cast, the priest's trained eye followed his every turn, numbered, as it were, the very steps he took. And the smile upon Frà Giovanni's face was fitful no more. He walked as a man who has a great jest for his company.

" Rocca the fool, and alone! They pay me a poor compliment, those new friends of mine ; but we shall repay, and the debt will be heavy."

He withdrew his hand from his habit, where it had rested upon the hilt of a dagger, for he knew that he had no need of any weapon. His gait was quick and careless ; he stopped often to peer into some window-less shop where a sickly lamp burned before the picture of a saint; and wares, which had not tempted a dead generation, appealed unavailingly to a living one. The idea that his very merriment might cost him his life never entered his head. He played with the assassin as a cat with a mouse, now tempting him to approach, now turning suddenly, and sending him helter-skelter into the door of a shop or the shadow of a bridge. He was sure of his man, and that certainty was a delight to him.

" If it had been any other but Rocca the clown ! " he said to himself, his thoughts ever upon the jest; " surely we shall know what to say to him."

He had come almost to the church of San Salvatore by this time. His walk had car-ried him out to the bank of a narrow, wind-

ing canal, at whose quays once-splendid gondolas were rotting in neglect. It seemed
to him that here was the place where his
tactics might well be changed and the *rôle* of
the hunted put aside for that of the hunter.
Quick to act, he stepped suddenly behind
one of the great wooden piles driven into the
quay for the warping of barges. The *bravo*,
who did not perceive that he had been de-
tected, and who could not account for the
sudden disappearance of his prey, came
straight on, his cloak wrapped about his
face, his naked sword in his hand. The wage
would be earned easily that night, he was
telling himself. No one would miss a beggarly monk — and he, Rocca, must live. A
single blow, struck to the right side of the
back, and then — and then —

This pleasant anticipation was cut short
abruptly by the total disappearance of the
man whose death was a preliminary to the
wage he anticipated so greedily. Mystified
beyond measure, he let his cloak fall back
again, and began to peer into the shadows as
though some miracle had been wrought and
the priest carried suddenly from earth to that
heaven whither he had meant to send him
so unceremoniously.

13

"Blood of Paul!" he exclaimed angrily, turning about and about again, "am I losing my eyes? A plague upon the place and the shadows."

He stamped his foot impotently, and was about to run back by the way he had come when a voice spoke in the shadows; and at the sound of the voice, the sword fell from the man's hand and he reeled back as from a blow.

"Rocca Zicani, the Prince is waiting for you."

The assassin staggered against the door of a house, and stood there as one paralysed. He had heard those words once before in the dungeons of Naples. They had been spoken by the Inquisitors who came to Italy with one of the Spanish princes. Instantly he recalled the scene where first he had listened to them, — the dungeon draped in black; the white-hot irons which had seared his flesh; the rack which had maimed his limbs, the masked men who had tortured him.

"Great God!" he moaned, " not that — not that — "

The priest stepped from the shadows and stood in a place where the feeble light of an oil lamp could fall upon his face. The laugh

"HE BEGAN TO PEER INTO THE SHADOWS."

hovered still about his lips. He regarded the trembling man with a contempt he would not conceal.

"Upon my word, Signor Rocca," he exclaimed, "this is a poor welcome to an old friend."

The *bravo*, who had fallen on his knees, for he believed that a trick had again delivered him into the hands of his enemies, looked up at the words, and stared at the monk as at an apparition.

"Holy Virgin!" he cried, "it is the Prince of Iseo."

The priest continued in the jester's tone:

"As you say, old comrade, the Prince of Iseo. Glory to God for the good fortune which puts you in my path to-night! Oh, you are very glad to see me, Signor Rocca, I'll swear to that. What, the fellow whom my hands snatched from the rack in the house of the Duke of Naples — has he no word for me? And he carries his naked sword in his hand; he has the face of a woman and his knees tremble. What means this?"

He had seemed to speak in jest, but while the cowed man was still kneeling before him, he, of a sudden, struck the sword aside, and, stooping, he gripped the *bravo* by the throat and dragged him from the shelter of the porch to the water's edge. As iron were the relentless hands; the man's eyes started from his head, the very breath seemed to be crushed out of him in the grip of the terrible priest.

"Signor Rocca, what means this?" the friar repeated. "A naked sword in your hand and sweat upon your brow. Oh, oh! a tale, indeed! Shall I read it to you, or shall I raise my voice and fetch those who will read it for me, — those who have the irons heated, and the boot so made for your leg that no last in Italy shall better it. Speak, rascal, shall I read you the tale?"

"Mercy, Prince, for the love of God!"

The priest released the pressure of his hands and let the other sink at his feet.

"Who sent you, rogue?" he asked. "Who pays your wage?"

"I dare not tell you, Excellency."

"Dare not! *you* dare not, — you, whom a word will put to torture greater than any you have dreamed of in your worst agonies; *you* dare not."

"Excellency, the Countess of Treviso; I am her servant."

"And the man who sent her to the work — his name?"

"Andrea, Count of Pisa, Excellency."

The priest stepped back as one whose curiosity was entirely satisfied.

"Ah! I thought so. And the price they paid you, knave?"

"Forty silver ducats, Excellency."

"Ho, ho! so that is the price of a friar in Venice."

The *bravo* sought to join in the jest.

"Had they known it was the Prince of Iseo, it had been a hundred thousand, Excellency."

Frà Giovanni did not listen to him. His quick brain was solving a strange problem, — the problem of the price that these people, in their turn, should pay to Venice. When he had solved it, he turned to the cringing figure at his feet.

"Signor Rocca," he said, "do you know of what I am thinking?"

"Of mercy, Excellency; of mercy for one who has not deserved it."

"But who can deserve it?"

"Excellency, hearken to me. I swear by all the saints —"

"In whose name you blaspheme, rascal.

Have I not heard your oath in Naples when the irons seared your flesh? Shall I listen again when the fire is being made ready, and there is burning coal beneath the bed you will lie upon to-night, Signor Rocca?"

"Oh! for God's sake, Excellency!"

"Not so; for the sake of Venice, rather."

"I will be your slave — I swear it on the cross — I will give my life — "

"Your precious life, Signor Rocca! — nay, what a profligate you are!"

Frà Giovanni's tone, perhaps, betrayed him. The trembling man began to take heart a little.

"Prove me, Excellency," he whined; "prove me here and now."

The friar made a pretence of debating it. After a little spell of silence he bade the other rise.

"Come," he said, "your legs catch cold, my friend, and will burn slowly. Stretch them here upon the Campo while I ask you some questions. And remember, for every lie you tell me there shall be another wedge in the boot you are about to wear. You understand that, signorè?"

"Excellency, the man that could lie to the Prince of Iseo has yet to be born."

It was a compliment spoken from the very heart; but the priest ignored it.

"Let us not speak of others, but of you and your friends. And, firstly, of the woman who sent you. She is now — "

"In the Palazzo Pisani waiting news of you."

"You were to carry that news to her?"

"And to receive my wage, Excellency. But I did not know what work it was — Holy God, I would not have come for — "

Frà Giovanni cut him short with a gesture of impatience.

"Tell me," he exclaimed, "the Count of Pisa, is he not the woman's lover?"

"They say so, signorè."

"And he is at her house to-night?"

The man shook his head.

"Before Heaven, I do not know, Excellency. An hour ago, he sat at a café in the great square."

"And the woman — was she alone when you left her?"

"There were three with her to sup."

The priest nodded his head.

"It is good!" he said; "we shall even presume to sup with her."

"To sup with her — but they will kill you, Excellency!"

" Ho, ho! see how this assassin is concerned for my life."

" Certainly I am. Have you not given me mine twice? I implore you not to go to the house —"

He would have said more, but the splash of an oar in the narrow canal by which they walked cut short his entreaties. A gondola was approaching them; the cry of the gondolier, awakening echoes beneath the eaves of the old houses, gave to Frà Giovanni that inspiration he had been seeking now for some minutes.

" Rocca Zicani," he exclaimed, standing suddenly as the warning cry, "*Stalè*," became more distinct, "I am going to put your professions to the proof."

" Excellency, I will do anything —"

" Then, if you would wake to-morrow with a head upon your shoulders, enter that gondola, and go back to those who sent you. Demand your wage of them —"

" But, Excellency —"

" Demand your wage of them," persisted the priest, sternly, "and say that the man who was their enemy lies dead before the church of San Salvatore. You understand me?"

"A GONDOLA WAS APPROACHING THEM."

A curious look came into the *bravo's* eyes.

"Saint John!" he cried, "that I should have followed such a one as you, Excellency!"

But the priest continued warningly:

"As you obey, so hope for the mercy of Venice. You deal with those who know how to reward their friends and to punish their enemies. Betray us, and I swear that no death in all Italy shall be such a death as you will die at dawn to-morrow."

He raised his voice, and summoned the gondolier to the steps of the quay. The *bravo* threw himself down upon the velvet cushions with the threat still ringing in his ears.

"Excellency," he said, "I understand. They shall hear that you are dead."

III

FRÀ GIOVANNI stepped from his gondola, and stood at the door of the Palazzo Pisani exactly at a quarter to ten o'clock. Thirty minutes had passed since he had talked with the *bravo*, Rocca, and had put him to the proof. The time was enough, he said; the tale would have been told, the glad news of

21

his own death already enjoyed by those who would have killed him.

Other men, perhaps, standing there upon the threshold of so daring an emprise, would have known some temptation of fear or hesitation in such a fateful moment; but the great Capuchin friar neither paused nor hesitated. That strange confidence in his own mission, his belief that God had called him to the protection of Venice, perchance even a personal conceit in his own skill as a swordsman, sent him hurrying to the work. It was a draught of life to him to see men tremble at his word; the knowledge which treachery poured into his ear was a study finer than that of all the manuscripts in all the libraries of Italy. And he knew that he was going to the Palazzo Pisani to humble one of the greatest in the city, — to bring the sons of Princes on their knees before him.

There were many lights in the upper storeys of the great house, but the ground floor, with its barred windows and cell-like chambers, was unlighted. The priest saw horrid faces grinning through the bars; the faces of fugitives, fleeing the justice of Venice, outcasts of the city, murderers. But these outcasts, in their turn, were silent

22

when they saw who came to the house, and they spoke of the strange guest in muted exclamations of surprise and wonder.

"Blood of Paul! do you see that? It is the Capuchin himself and alone. Surely there will be work to do anon."

"Ay, but does he come alone? Saint John! I would sooner slit a hundred throats than have his shadow fall on me. Was it not he that hanged Orso and the twelve! A curse upon the day he came to Venice."

So they talked in whispers, but the priest had passed already into the great hall of the palace and was speaking to a lackey there.

"My friend," he said, "I come in the name of the Signori. If you would not hear from them to-morrow, announce me to none."

The lackey drew back, quailing before the threat.

"Excellency," he exclaimed, "I am but a servant — "

"And shall find a better place as you serve Venice faithfully."

He passed on with noiseless steps, mounting the splendid marble staircase upon which the masterpieces of Titian and of Paolo Veronese looked down. At the head of the stairs, there was a painted door, which he had but to open to find himself face to face with those who were still telling each other that he was dead.

For an instant, perhaps, a sense of the danger of his mission possessed him. He knew well that one false step, one word undeliberated, would be paid for with his own blood. But even in the face of this reckoning he did not hesitate. He was there to save Venice from her enemies; the God of Venice would protect him. And so without word or warning, he opened the door and stood, bold and unflinching, before those he had come to accuse.

There were four at table, and one was a woman. The priest knew her well. She had been called the most beautiful woman in Venice, — Catherine, Countess of Treviso. Still young, with a face which spoke of ambition and of love, her white neck glittered with the jewels it carried, her dress of blue velvet was such a dress as only a noblewoman of Venice could wear. A queenly figure, the friar said, yet one he would so humble presently that never should she hold up her head again.

As for the others, the men who had cloaked conspiracy with a woman's smile, he would know how to deal with them. Indeed, when he scanned their faces and began to remember the circumstances under which he had met them before, his courage was strengthened, and he forgot that he had ever reasoned with it.

He stood in the shadows; but the four, close in talk, and thinking that a lackey had entered the room, did not observe him. They were laughing merrily at some jest, and filling the long goblets with the golden wine of Cyprus, when at last he strode out into the light and spoke to them. His heart beat quickly; he knew that this might be the hour of his death, yet never had his voice been more sonorous or more sure.

"Countess," he exclaimed, as he stepped boldly to the table and confronted them, "I bring you a message from Andrea, the lord of Pisa!"

He had expected that the woman would cry out, or that the men would leap to their feet and draw their swords; but the supreme moment passed and no one spoke. A curious silence reigned in the place. From without there floated up the gay notes of a gondolier's carol. The splash of oars was heard, and the low murmur of voices. But within the room you could have counted the tick of a watch — almost the beating of a man's heart. And the woman was the first to find her tongue. She had looked at the friar as she would have looked at the risen dead; but, suddenly, with an effort which brought back the blood to her cheeks, she rose from her seat and began to speak.

"Who are you?" she asked; "and why do you come to this house?"

Frà Giovanni advanced to the table so that they could see his face.

"Signora," he said, "the reason of my coming to this house I have already told you. As to your other question, I am the Capuchin friar, Giovanni, whom you desired your servant Rocca to kill at the church of San Salvatore an hour ago."

The woman sank back into the chair; the blood left her face; she would have swooned had not curiosity proved stronger than her terror.

"The judgment of God!" she cried.

Again, for a spell, there was silence in the room. The priest stood at the end of the table telling himself that he must hold these four in talk until the bells of San Luca struck ten o'clock, or pay for failure with his life.

The men, in their turn, were asking themselves if he were alone.

"You are the Capuchin friar, Giovanni," exclaimed one of them presently, taking courage of the silence, "what, then, is your message from the Count of Pisa?"

"My message, signorè, is this, — that at ten o'clock to-night, the Count of Pisa will have ceased to live."

A strange cry, terrible in its pathos, escaped the woman's lips. All had risen to their feet again. The swords of the three leaped from their scabbards. The instant of the priest's death seemed at hand. But he stood, resolute, before them.

"At ten o'clock," he repeated sternly, "the Count of Pisa will have ceased to live. That is his message, signori, to one in this house. And to you, the Marquis of Cittadella, there is another message."

He turned to one of the three who had begun to rail at him, and raised his hand as in warning. So great was the curiosity to hear his words that the swords were lowered again, and again there could be heard the ticking of a clock in the great room.

"For me — a message! Surely I am favoured, signorè."

"Of that you shall be the judge, since, at dawn to-morrow, your head will lie on the marble slab between the columns of the Piazzetta."

They greeted him with shouts of ridicule.

" A prophet — a prophet!"

" A prophet indeed," he answered quietly, "who has yet a word to speak to you, Andrea Foscari."

" To me!" exclaimed the man addressed, who was older than the others, and who wore the stola of the nobility.

" Ay, to you, who are about to become a fugitive from the justice of Venice. Midnight shall see you hunted in the hills, my lord ; no house shall dare to shelter you; no hand shall give you bread. When you return to the city you would have betrayed, the very children shall mock you for a beggar."

Foscari answered with an oath, and drew back. The third of the men, a youth who wore a suit of white velvet, and whose vest was ablaze with gold and jewels, now advanced jestingly.

" And for me, most excellent friar?"

" For you, Gian Mocenigo, a pardon in the name of that Prince of Venice whose house you have dishonoured."

Again they replied to him with angry gibes.

"A proof — a proof — we will put you to the proof, friar — here and now, or, by God, a prophet shall pay with his life."

He saw that they were driven to the last point. While the woman stood as a figure of stone at the table, the three advanced towards him and drove him back before their threatening swords. The new silence was the silence of his death anticipated. He thought that his last word was spoken in vain. Ten o'clock would never strike, he said. Yet even as hope seemed to fail him, and he told himself that the end had come, the bells of the city began to strike the hour, and the glorious music of their echoes floated over the sleeping waters.

"A proof, you ask me for a proof, signori," he exclaimed triumphantly. "Surely, the proof lies in yonder room, where all the world may see it."

He pointed to a door opening in the wall of mirrors, and giving access to a smaller chamber. Curiosity drove the men thither. They threw open the door; they entered the room; they reeled back drunk with their own terror.

For the body of Andrea, lord of Pisa, lay,

still warm, upon the marble pavement of the chamber, and the dagger with which he had been stabbed was yet in his heart.

" A proof — have I not given you a proof?" the priest cried again, while the woman's terrible cry rang through the house, and the three stood close together, as men upon whom a judgment has fallen.

" Man or devil — who are you?" they asked in hushed whispers.

He answered them by letting his monk's robe slip from his shoulders. As the robe fell, they beheld a figure clad in crimson velvet and corselet of burnished gold; the figure of a man whose superb limbs had been the envy of the swordsmen of Italy; whose face, lighted now with a sense of power and of victory, was a face for which women had given their lives.

" It is the Prince of Iseo," they cried, and, saying it, fled from the house of doom.

At that hour, those whose gondolas were passing the Palazzo Pisani observed a strange spectacle. A priest stood upon the balcony of the house holding a silver lamp in his hand; and as he waited, a boat emerged from the shadows about the church of San Luca and came swiftly towards him.

"THE BODY OF ANDREA, COUNT OF PISA, LAY UPON THE MARBLE PAVEMENT."

THE RISEN DEAD

"The Signori of the Night," the loiterers exclaimed in hushed whispers, and went on their way quickly.

.   .   .   .   .

Very early next morning, a rumour of strange events, which had happened in Venice during the hours of darkness, drew a great throng of the people to the square before the ducal palace.

"Have you not heard it," man cried to man, — "the Palazzo Pisani lacks a mistress to-day? The police make their toilet in the boudoir of my lady. And they say that the lord of Pisa is dead."

"Worse than that, my friends," a gondolier protested, "Andrea Foscari crossed to Maestre last night, and the dogs are even now on his heels."

"Your news grows stale," croaked a hag who was passing; "go to the Piazzetta and you shall see the head of one who prayed before the altar ten minutes ago."

They trooped off, eager for the spectacle. When they reached the Piazzetta, the hag was justified. The head of a man lay bleeding upon the marble slab between the columns. It was the head of the Marquis of Cittadella.

THE SIGNORS OF THE NIGHT

In the palace of the police, meanwhile, Pietro Falier, the Captain, was busy with his complaints.

"The lord of Pisa is dead," he said; "the woman has gone to the Convent of Murano; there is a head between the columns; Andrea Foscari will die of hunger in the hills, — yet Gian Mocenigo goes free. Who is this friar that he shall have the gift of life or death in Venice?"

His subordinate answered, —

"This friar, Captain, is one whom Venice, surely, will make the greatest of her nobles to-day."

A SERMON FOR CLOWNS

I

ON the morning of the feast of the Ascension, in the year 1702, Scavezzo, the fat Canon of St. Mark's, stood before the booth of old Barbarino, the clown, and rated its owner soundly.

"What!" he cried; "to mock a Canon of the Ducal House, to hold him up to the ridicule of the people, to ape his sermons and his gestures. Out on you for a rogue who shall be whipped before dawn to-morrow!"

It was obvious to the densest person that the good churchman was exceedingly angry. What with his loud and penetrating voice, the menace of his gold-topped staff, and the meek and humble attitude of old Barbarino, all the people on the Piazzetta came running up to the booth, — some to take the part of the clown; some to show their loyalty, for reasons of profit, to the colossal and unwieldy churchman. Even gondoliers left their boats at the neighbouring quay to learn the cause of the clamour; while over yonder, at the cafés, on the Piazza, gallants and great dames ceased their chatter to listen to the brawl.

"Excellency," said the clown, bowing humbly before the Canon's wrath, "I beg you to listen to me. I hope that I know who I am. If I am little and you are big — "

The crowd roared with merriment at the unhappy slip. As for the fat preacher, he positively shook with anger.

"How! You insult me, rogue! here at the door of my own church! But I must teach you a lesson. I must show you that there is still justice in Venice for her church-men. Wait until the whip falls upon your shoulders; you shall tell me then if I am big or no."

The poor clown, terrified by his threats, wrung his hands in despair.

"Oh! a thousand pardons, Excellency!" he exclaimed. "I am sorry for my words. I should have said that you are — "

"Enormous," cried someone in the mob.

The Canon strode from the booth and shook his stick at them.

"To-morrow," he said dramatically, "to-morrow not one stone of this house shall remain upon another."

The crowd roared anew at the sally. Venice was never a great respecter of her priests, and Venice loved old Barbarino, the clown, — principally, perhaps, for the sake of his daughter Nina, the prettiest dancing girl in all the city.

"By Bacchus!" cried a merry gondolier. "Not one stone upon another, eh, and the house built of wood? A miracle, your Excellency, a miracle!"

"Do not disturb his Excellency's thoughts," chimed in a second; "he is about to give us his blessing."

"Not at all," said a third. "His Excellency is not very well to-day. Was it not a black fast yesterday, my friends, and did not the good Canon keep it on three capons and a boar's head? A plague on you for slanderers of a holy man!"

But Scavezzo, the fat Canon, was already out of hearing. Bristling with anger, his vanity sore wounded, he had gone at once to the police, and had laid his complaint before them. They obeyed him promptly.

Within an hour there came to old Barbarino the intimation that, at dawn to-morrow, he and his must leave the city.

In vain the old man pleaded with the Chief of the Police that for ten years he had been as much a part of Venice as the Patriarch himself; in vain he recalled the honours which great men had heaped on his head, the licence they had permitted him. No word of his was allowed to prevail above that of so mighty a personage as a Canon of St. Mark's. At dawn to-morrow he must go.

Never was there assembled in any booth a company of clowns so melancholy as those gathered in the booth of old Barbarino that afternoon. Punchinello, Columbine, Harlequin — tears were upon the cheeks of them all. To quit Venice, — their home; to wander as beggars on the high-road of Italy! Not to know whence their bread would come or straw for their pillows! And all this for a word against a beggarly canon whom Venice could well spare, ay, and a dozen of their kind. No surprise, then, that the feast of the Ascension, the great feast, meant nothing to the clowns. Their day was done; others would enjoy their triumphs and eat their bread.

Little Nina, the dancing girl, listened to

these doleful complaints, but did not share them. She loved Venice, though she was but sixteen years old, loved the city as well as those who beat and starved her and robbed her of the *scudi* that her talent earned. She had a good wit of her own, too, and when old Barbarino returned from the palace with tears in his eyes, she nodded her pretty head cunningly, and crept from the booth unheeded and unobserved.

Half-an-hour later, she had crossed the canal in her own little gondola and had reached the house of one who, in all but name, was then the first man in Venice, — Frà Giovanni, the Capuchin friar, whose pity for children was as the pity of the Master who sent him to the work.

There were many waiting to speak to the great priest, noble women and senators and even the captains of the police, but when he came out from his library and saw the clown's daughter waiting timidly in his ante-room, he beckoned to her before them all and at once asked her for her news.

" Well," he said, shutting the door of the library upon a great dame who would have thrust her way in with the young girl, " and what is little Nina's trouble to-day?"

"Oh, Excellency," she cried, holding his hand in both of hers, "we have no longer a home in Venice; we are to leave at dawn. God help us; we shall have to beg our bread!"

Frà Giovanni sat in his big chair, and stroked her pretty hair.

"They beat you and starve you—and yet you speak of begging your bread. Would that be so great a hardship, little Nina?"

"Excellency," she said simply, "I love Venice; it is the only home I have ever known. And for my father's sake—oh, I know that you will help us. It was yesterday,—the day of fast. My father preached to the people, and the people said he was Scavezzo, the Canon of St. Mark's. Oh, Excellency, if you could have heard them laugh. And now we are to be punished; the police say so; we are to sleep in our booth no more—and all because the Canon is fat, Excellency, oh, so fat, and my father wore a sack at his girth—and you know—"

She stopped for very want of breath. A curious smile spread over the face of the friar. He continued to stroke her hair in silence. Her heart beat quick, for she knew that he would help her.

38

"So it is Scavezzo, the Canon, who complains, Nina. The people laughed, you say?"

"You could not hear yourself speak, Excellency. Oh, they do not love Scavezzo; they would not wish us to leave them. And Venice is so dear to us — you will not send us away, Excellency?"

Frà Giovanni shook his head doubtingly.

"Who am I, Nina, that the police should listen to me?"

"You are the friend of the friendless, Excellency."

"And you think that the Canon will hear me?"

She bowed her head, for she could not answer him.

"What shall I do if you will not help me, Excellency?" she exclaimed.

He did not answer her for a little while. Some scheme seemed running in his mind. When he spoke again, the smile was still upon his face.

"Come," he said cheerily, "we must dry up those tears. Tell me, would your father be at his booth if I went there now?"

"He would say that God sent you, Excellency."

Again the priest seemed lost in thought. But it was not to be hidden from her that his thoughts amused him.

"Well," he said, rising from his chair presently, "we are going to see your father, Nina. And while we go, you will be on your way to Murano. You know the church of San Pietro there?"

"As I know your house, Excellency!"

"And the home of Michael, the woodcarver — you have been there, Nina!"

She thought upon it a little and then answered, —

"Michael, the wood-carver — but, Excellency, he is as fat as Scavezzo himself; you could not tell one from the other."

A great light burst upon her. She began to clap her hands joyfully.

"Oh, Excellency," she cried, "you are going to save us, then!"

"Before vespers to-morrow, little Nina, Scavezzo, the Canon, shall ask pardon of you on his knees."

She kissed his hand rapturously; but the priest drew his cowl about his face, and, regardless of those who waited for him, set out upon his way to the booth of Barbarino, the clown.

A SERMON FOR CLOWNS

II

Scavezzo, the fat Canon of St. Mark's, kept the feast of the Ascension right well. All day long there had been the clash of silver bells from the steeples of Venice, the thunder of cannon from her forts. Measureless processions had passed through the square before the great church on their way to witness the wedding of the Adriatic. Nobles in splendid robes of silk and velvet, deacons bearing tapers, captains of the city in scarlet, chancellors, equerries, beautiful women glittering in jewels, the Doge himself in ermine and blue and cloth of gold, — all these, in gondolas decked out with gaudy draperies and weighed down with flowers, had gone out once more to wed that sea which Venice had ruled so long.

And when night fell, and there was music of fifes and the strings were tuned in every house, and the city put on a dazzling raiment of countless lanterns, the people had their turn, and hurried in their thousands to welcome the people's procession upon the Piazza, — to assist in a masquerade surpassing anything known in all the history of carnival.

Scavezzo, the fat Canon, was supping when

this second procession emerged from the church; but his faithful servant, Giacomo, stood at the window of the presbytery, and gave him constant news of it. Not for such a trifle as the most splendid pageant in all Europe would Scavezzo turn from a grinning boar's head or a goblet filled to the brim with the luscious wine of Cyprus. Processions, — he had taken part in those all day. And that fat *poulet*, his mouth watered at the steaming odour of it. A fig for the people and their pleasures when a canon supped.

"They are coming, you say, Giacomo; then who carries the cross before them?"

"Gabrino, the clerk — he walks like a prince, my master. And there are a hundred priests behind him. Body of Mark! there is cloth of gold enough down yonder to hang the walls of a city. Hark to the roll of the drums! It is like thunder in the hills."

Scavezzo took a large piece of meat upon his fork and surveyed it with great satisfaction.

"And behind the priests — who walk behind the priests, Giacomo?"

"Two hundred and fifty with torches, your Excellency. It is night made day. The eyes are blinded with the fire. And lanterns,

Saint Paul, who shall count the lanterns I see?"

Scavezzo ate the dainty morsel and smacked his lips in token of his satisfaction.

"It is good!" he sighed; and then, "there will be the women of the city, too, Giacomo."

Giacomo leered pleasantly.

"They have come down from Paradise, Excellency; never were such women seen. Your Reverence does well to turn your eyes away."

The fat Canon groaned inaudibly; he emptied his goblet at a draught.

"Let us not speak of them, Giacomo. let us remember to mortify —"

His platitude, doubtlessly good, was cut short by a new exclamation from the old servant at the window.

"Ho! ho!" he said, "here come the clowns! I see Barbarino, the fool, and little Nina, the dancing girl. And there is Harlequin — legs of a thousand devils, I can hear the laughter now. Were there ever such fellows in all the world, and faithful servants of Holy Church, too, your Excellency!"

Scavezzo, recalled suddenly to a memory of the morning, ground his teeth.

"To-morrow," he said to himself, "to-morrow there will be one booth the less in Venice."

But Giacomo continued, unconscious of his master's anger, —

"A plague upon the banners which hide them from my sight, Excellency, for there is Il Magnifico himself, and the Doctor in his Bologna gown, and the lovers at the play. Saint John, if all the love in Venice were made like that! But I must not ask your Reverence to be an authority on such a point."

He continued to grin and to leer as the love play went on in the vast square below. Scavezzo, meanwhile, had brought his supper to an abrupt conclusion. The memory of the clowns was as vinegar upon his meat. He said that he would wake to-morrow to hear that Barbarino and his daughter, Nina, had gone, bag and baggage, to the mainland. And with this happy assurance to give him peace, he called to Giacomo to bring his coffee.

"You are growing deaf in your old age, Giacomo. Coffee, my friend, coffee."

To his infinite surprise, the old man at the window did not answer a single word. Rather he stood as one petrified, now looking to the square below, now at his master.

His face was contorted strangely. Some horrible apparition appeared to have so affected his visage that his eyes stood out like eyes of glass, and the veins of his forehead were full to bursting.

"Oh, my master — oh, for Heaven's sake — what is it that I see!"

The fat Canon leant back in his chair and surveyed his servant with contempt.

"Giacomo," he said, "how often have I told you that your stomach is too old for the red wine of Vicenza — ?"

The rebuke fell upon deaf ears. The old servant remained indifferent alike to his master's question and to his scorn. He stood at the window drunk indeed, but drunk with terror.

"How!" he cried with a terrible laugh, "two masters, — one here and one there. Oh, saints and angels defend us!"

Scavezzo raised himself with an effort from his chair.

"Giacomo," he exclaimed, "you are certainly drunk. To-morrow you shall fast on bread and water, and then your eyesight will be better. Meanwhile, we will see — "

The threat was checked abruptly upon the Canon's lips. He, too, was at the window now; he looked down upon the Piazza below; he heard the merry music; he saw the countless lights, the gay dresses, the tremendous throng of masqueraders; above all, he saw — himself!

Scavezzo rocked upon his heels as a man struck suddenly with dizziness. He wondered no longer that Giacomo had not answered him. He, the Canon of St. Mark's Chapel; he, the great preacher; he, the admired ecclesiastic upon whom the women of Venice fawned, was he drunk also, was he in his room or out there on the Piazza; had some cunning drug in his wine made him see double? The very room seemed to swim before him. He gasped for breath and unloosed his cassock at the throat.

"I am Scavezzo," he cried hoarsely, "who, in God's name, then, is that other?"

Old Giacomo crossed himself devoutly.

"My master," he exclaimed, "we are bewitched. A woman stood at the altar this morning, and she had the evil eye. That is why I see you in the square down yonder, when in reality you are at supper in this room. And look — you sit upon a golden chair, there is a fool's cap on your head, you have a flagon in your hand, a woman —

46

" ' OH, MY MASTER—OH, FOR HEAVEN'S SAKE—
WHAT IS IT THAT I SEE!' "

that I should say it — a woman sits upon your knee — oh, Excellency, was ever such a thing heard of since the blessed saint came to Venice."

But it was Scavezzo's turn to be deaf now. The ringing shouts of the masqueraders in the square moved him to a frenzy such as he had never known. One thing only was clear to him, and it was this, that out there, on the Piazza, seated upon a chair of gold, which strong arms carried, and mumming that the people might laugh, was his double, his other self, a man so like him in face and feature, and in vast unwieldy bulk, that his own father might have been perplexed to say which was which.

How the man came there, what devilry prompted him to wear the cassock and bands of a Canon of St. Mark's, the terrified ecclesiastic dare not ask himself. He had but one idea, — he must stop the procession at any cost, he must expose an impostor, he must go out and cry to the people : " Here is the true Scavezzo; here is the Canon to whose pulpit you come!"

The idea quickened his laborious step as never it had been quickened before. Deft were the fat fingers which buttoned up his purple cape.   Heavy was his breathing as he put on his great hat with the broad brim, and shuffled into the shoes with the silver buckles, and grasped his staff, and repeated to his stupefied servant the assurance that justice should be done.

" To-morrow, Giacomo, to-morrow he shall know the whip and the iron. What! to hold me up before the people with a flagon in my hand and a fool's cap on my head! God's law! the police shall have a word to say about that!"

Giacomo, trembling still, sought to hold him back.

"My master," he implored, "you will not go among them to-night. Hark to those cries — they are like the cries of wild beasts. If you value your life — "

Scavezzo did not heed him. His hand shook with passion. Giacomo said afterwards that he descended his staircase with steps which made the house quake. He must stop the procession! He must pull the buffoon, who was his other self, from the throne whereon the clowns had placed him! Never must Venice be left to believe that a Canon of St. Mark's had so disgraced himself. The mere determination gave him a nerve of iron. A man of quick temper, his mind dwelt lovingly upon the punishment to-morrow should bring upon the miscreants who had mocked him. They should be burnt with irons, he said; and so saying, he opened the door of the presbytery and passed into the great square.

For some minutes the dazzling lights, the roar of voices, the wail of fifes, the rolling of drums, made him feel as one tossed suddenly into an angry sea. Everywhere about him masqueraders were moving. Strange figures with hideous visages, pretty women on the arms of lovers, jesters, monks, sailors, priests, mingled headlong in that tremendous throng. Nevertheless, one cry prevailed loud above all others. It was the welcome of the mob to the man in the golden chair,—to the man the people believed to be Scavezzo, the Canon of St. Mark's.

" *Viva,. viva !* Long life to our Father Scavezzo! Another flagon for his hand, another cap for his head. *Viva, viva !* a Canon of canons! And yon is Dorimene on his lap — oh, *viva, viva !* "

Scavezzo heard the cries, and they were as blows upon his ears. He began to hasten with all the speed he could command towards

4

the Piazzetta, and as he ran, a man, masked in red and wearing a scarlet dress, followed close upon his steps, and at length made bold to touch him on the arm.

"What think you of this sight, my father," cried the stranger, "a holy Canon of St. Mark's masquerading like a juggler from Normandy. Was ever such a thing known in Venice?"

Scavezzo turned to the stranger eagerly.

"My friend," he said, "a very great wrong has been done this night. I am Scavezzo, the true Canon of the Ducal Chapel. Who that fellow may be, I cannot tell you. Help me, I pray, to speak to the people."

The man in the red mask, thus addressed, surveyed the trembling ecclesiastic as one who has heard a fairy story.

"The devil!" said he, "when I come to look at you, my father, there is truth in your words. You are a kinsman, perhaps, and the disgrace of your famous relative wounds you. I approve your charity. Let us go together and protest before this astounding canon, who, upon my word, is little credit to Venice."

The Canon wrung his hands; his grief was pitiable to see.

"Oh," he said, "that I should not be myself, that there should be two of us — am I going mad?"

The stranger answered him by linking arms with him and leading him deeper into the whirling throng.

"Come along, then," he cried encouragingly. "It is not you who are mad, my friend, but that dolt of a relative of yours who certainly must have lost his wits. I wonder that the police do not interfere. Hark to his jests! Did ever such words fall from the lips of a churchman before? And, as I live — he is eating a capon as big as himself. Shame on the rogue to forget his office so!"

A tremendous shout of laughter from the people bore testimony to the truth of the masked man's word. Scavezzo, as short as he was fat, made painful efforts to stand upon the tips of his toes; but so great was the press about him that he could see nothing.

"Oh," he wailed, "what an infamy — I that have a woman's appetite!"

The stranger laughed until the tears came into his merry eyes.

"Ha! ha! ha! They have handed him a second capon as big as an eagle. He is putting it in the sack at his girth. You can see him swelling, father. And now, by the barrel of Bacchus, he sits down upon his chair, the chair flies into a hundred pieces, and the Canon's heels are in the air. Oh, shame, shame, — I laugh like a girl."

Scavezzo clenched his hands until the long nails penetrated the flesh.

" My friends," he roared, seeking to make his voice heard above the tumult, " do not look at him — here is the true Scavezzo. Come and see him for yourself — come and touch him. That fellow there is an impostor. Do not hear him. Listen to me, I implore you."

He might as well have spoken to the walls of the arsenal. The mob was in a frenzy of delight now.

" *Viva, viva !* " it was screaming; " Scavezzo dances for us. Oh, the great Scavezzo! To-morrow there will be ten thousand about his pulpit. Oh, the holy man, the wonder ! "

The fervid cries were drowned in the hoarse shouts of laughter with which the new performance was greeted. The false Canon of St. Mark's was dancing before the people. There was no doubt at all about it.

The thunder of his feet upon the throne which carried him was as the roll of some tremendous drum. The true Canon, obtaining a moment's glimpse of the spectacle, nearly fainted at it.

" Oh, for the love of God," he cried to the stranger at his side, " help me and save me, signorè. Who am I, where am I? Is it another that speaks to you or Scavezzo the Canon? Oh, in the name of charity!"

The stranger gripped his arm yet tighter.

" Come," he said, " this wanton exhibition has unhinged your mind, father. We will go to the police, and see if they permit such disgraceful sights in their city. A Canon dancing in a booth like a common harlequin. What an example for the people!"

He spoke with a fine assumption of anger, and Scavezzo, in his turn, permitted himself to be dragged through the outer ranks of the delighted crowd; but his cassock was torn as he went, and he groaned often.

" I have never danced in all my life," he protested piteously; " God did not make me to dance. It is true that I drank a little red wine with my meat, but a flagon like that, as big as the dome of a church, it is monstrous, it is cruel, signorè!"

The stranger dragged him on, regardless of his distress.

"Courage," he said, "we are going to the police. Trust them to right a wrong, father. To-morrow all Venice shall hear that Scavezzo, the Canon, is in the dungeons of the palace."

The Canon laughed ironically, hysterically.

"I am another, then," he exclaimed; "this morning I was Scavezzo, but Scavezzo is dead. He dances on a barrel, and there is a fool's cap on his head. And to-morrow, the dungeon! God help me, the dungeon!"

The man in the mask pretended not to hear him. He had helped the fat Canon across the square, and should have turned to the right to find the offices of the police; but instead of that, he turned to the left, and plunged at once into that maze of narrow streets they call the Merceria. There, at a little wine-shop, above which was the sign of a Turk's head, he stopped as though a new idea had come to him.

"Father," he said, "I am thinking that we are in no fit state to present ourselves to the Captain of the Police just now. Enter here, where they will give us a glass of wine, and even a needle for your cassock. When the wine is drunk, we can go across to the palace and tell our tale."

Scavezzo assented willingly. He could still hear the frenzied shouts ringing across the piazza. A ribald chorus, a haunting, vulgar lilt had been taken up by the people, and its echoes floated across the sleeping lagoon, and were heard by the distant islanders.

" Oh," he said, " hark to that. The fellow is teaching them to sing a ribald song against our Lord, the Pope. I know it well, signorè."

The stranger dragged him into the shop.

" I fear your kinsman will hang, after all," he said grimly. " Drink a glass of wine, father, and then — to the police."

Scavezzo obeyed him as a child. He scarce knew who he was or where he was. The little wine-shop would have been in darkness but for the scanty rays of light emitted by an old brass lamp burning before an image. He could not see the face of the hag who came out to serve him. His hand trembled as he lifted the glass to his lips, and no sooner had he put it down than the drug which it contained began to act, and he fell senseless into the arms of the man who had brought him to the shop.

"Quick," said the unknown, as other masked men came to his assistance, "he must wake at Murano in the house of Michael, the wood-carver."

III

THE sun had been shining hotly upon the Island of Murano for many hours when Scavezzo, the Canon, awoke from his heavy sleep. It had been a troubled sleep, bringing him curious dreams; and chiefly a dream in which he saw himself preaching to a congregation of clowns, and must, in spite of himself, make jokes for their amusement. When he awoke at last with throbbing temples and burning face, he called loudly for Giacomo, his servant, and began to fear that he would be late for Mass.

"Giacomo, Giacomo — do you not hear me? Water, rascal, and my cassock — quick!"

Now, the Canon's eyes were hardly opened when he said this; and what was his astonishment, a moment later, to find himself, not in his own presbytery, as he thought, but lying upon a low wooden bed in a long narrow room which he had never

56

seen before, and whose very furniture was of a kind to awe him. Everywhere strange, inanimate figures gaped at him, — here a monster, half man, half dragon; there a figure of a centaur; here, a scene from purgatory richly carved in wood; there, a fantastic group of demons designed for the staircase of some rich merchant, — an odd assortment, in truth, which, seen in the dim light of the room, might well have startled one of stronger nerves than Scavezzo, the Canon. And to say that the Canon was merely startled would be to misrepresent his story altogether. For minutes together he glared at the hideous, grinning, voiceless things, as at an army of spectres risen from the ground before him.

"Oh," he said, " wake up, Scavezzo ; wake up. This is your dream; you are sleeping still, and that rogue of a Giacomo has forgotten to call you. You will be late for Mass, Scavezzo, and what will the Patriarch say ? "

He laughed a little nervously as he spoke, and sat bolt upright in his bed. His mind was strangely confused; but gradually it began to bring back to him the mysterious doings of last night. A procession around the Piazza! — yes, he remembered that. And afterwards, supper, and a man in a scarlet mask, and a great throng of masqueraders, and someone singing ribald songs about the Pope.

Round and round in his head the strange figures of thought went, until, in a moment of quaking terror, the figures fell into line and the whole scene was played over again for him. In that instant he remembered all, — the false Scavezzo, the man on the golden chair, the fool's cap, the flagon, the ringing cheers of the mob, his own overwhelming, imperishable disgrace.

" Great God!" he cried, " it was true, then. I did not dream it. There was another Scavezzo in the square. He did dance that the people might laugh. And now, holy patron, where am I now? What has brought me to this place? In whose house am I?"

He waddled to the door, for he had slept in his clothes; and opened it with uncertain hands. The sun's rays streamed into the room and half blinded him; but when his eyes mastered the light, he could see a great expanse of water, and in the distance the golden domes of Venice and of his own church. He knew then that the low house stood upon the quay of some island, and that he was alone in it. It was a glorious day, and many a gondolier went by singing a merry song. One of them, resting upon his oar, spoke to the Canon, and the words were the strangest Scavezzo had ever heard.

"How! Michael, and who brought you home from carnival?" cried the man.

Scavezzo drew himself up proudly.

"Impudent fellow," he said, "do you not see to whom you are talking?"

The man roared with laughter.

"Behold!" said he, "am I not talking to Michael, the wood-carver, who came home last night with his heels where his head should have been? Shame on him for a guzzling rogue that has forgotten the name he bears."

The Canon shook his fist at him, and turned angrily from the water's edge. He had not thought of the clothes he wore, but now he looked at them, and perceived to his astonishment that he was arrayed no more in spotless violet cassock and shoes with the silver buckles. These had given place to a suit of coarse brown cloth, with boots such as only the common workmen buy. Moreover, a leather belt was about his waist, and in this belt a workman's knife was sheathed. For quite a long time the Canon stood at the door of the house, shaking his head, as one who is perplexed beyond understanding.

"I wear a suit of brown clothes, and wake in a house I have never seen," he said, continuing to nod his head mechanically. "A boatman calls me Michael, and insults me. I am upon the Island of Murano, and I can see my home across the water. Has someone robbed me of my senses, then? Do I sleep still? Am I gone mad in a night? I will believe no such thing. I will believe — "

The voices of children, who ran up suddenly to the place where he stood, cut short the expression of his will. As a rule, he was, like other fat men, benevolent and well disposed to the little ones; and when these children came up to him, he greeted them very kindly.

"My children," he asked, "do you know whose house this is, and where the owner may be found?"

Their response was a merry shout; they went scampering away, crying to one another: "Here is old Michael, the wood-

carver, drunk with wine! Oh, come and
see; come and see!"

Scavezzo suppressed the evil words that
came even to his lips. He looked down
again at his poor brown clothes, up again at
the house wherein he had slept.

"I am bewitched," he murmured; "this is
the reward of my sins — Heaven pity me!
I am no longer myself; I am someone else.
Scavezzo is dead. He is Michael, the wood-
carver! Oh, cursed day!"

Muttering thus, with dizzy head and weak
limbs, he began to stagger rather than to
walk along to the quay towards the great
church of the island. The priest there
would know him, he thought; perchance
would lend him a cassock, and find a gondolier to take him home. The possibility gave
him some little hope; but he had not gone
very far before the children, who had cried
out upon him, came running back again,
and brought with them others, shrewish
women and idle men, who had come to see
the unusual spectacle of a drunken wood-
carver. These gave him hard words and
many a push; and presently a crowd began
to gather, and to jeer at him.

"Ho, ho! thou art drunk still, old Michael.

Have a care, rogue, or they will put thee in the pillory."

"Shame on him, for a lazy rascal that lets his children starve, and beats his good wife!"

"Ay, thou dost well to speak of his wife. Wait until she comes back from Torcello. A right good arm has Antonina, and well she knows how to use it."

The suggestion was the last infamy. At the word "wife" old Scavezzo raised his arms as though to beat off the devils who tormented him.

"Wife!" he roared. "You speak to me of a wife! Do you not know, then, who I am? Do you not see that I am Scavezzo, the Canon of St. Mark's? Scoffers, I will have you whipped — I will have you — "

Anger choked his utterance. He stumbled on blindly towards the church. The crowd increased and began to hoot him, until his ears rang with the clamour and the din.

"Oh, come and see; come and see! Here is a wood-carver whom the bottle has made a Canon! Oh, come and see!"

But above this cry was another, and it was more ominous.

"To the pillory with him, and learn there what sort of a Canon he is."

New-comers took up the new word, and it was repeated with loud shouts of joy. Some laid hands upon the Canon's arm, some pushed, some pulled him. His piteous appeals for mercy fell upon ears that wished to be deaf. The louder he protested that he was Scavezzo, the wilder were the cries: "A wood-carver that has gone mad — oh, come and see!"

On they dragged him, past the church which was to have been his sanctuary, away from the water and the ships, onward to the open square of the island, even to the pillory, where ready hands strapped his arms, and readier urchins prepared their ammunition.

"A leek for thy stomach, old Michael."

"An apple for thy head."

"Water to wash the wine out of thee, old man."

"A stinking fish to remind thee of Lent."

"The half of an egg to keep up thy strength."

"A dead dog, old Michael, to whom thou mayest preach."

So the delighted mob roared as it gathered round the pillory and began to amuse itself.

Savage cries of delight accompanied the bombardment. The square of the island was

filled by a vast throng which hooted incessantly, and always invited others to come and
see the wood-carver of whom good wine had
made a Canon. Even in distant Venice the
clamour was heard, and the report believed
that Murano was in arms. As for Scavezzo
himself, he had the mind neither to think
nor to protest any more. The ultimate
humiliation had overtaken him. Whatever
the years might have in store for him, this
must remain, that he, the darling Canon of
the women of Venice, had stood in a pillory
on the Island of Murano. He could have
prayed to God that the earth would open
and swallow him up.

Throughout that long afternoon, the man
who had sworn to banish the clowns from
Venice, was the mock and the sport of the
islanders. Yet strange it was that no serious
hurt befell him; and still more strange that
at sunset the crowd seemed to melt away as
if by magic, and he was left alone in that
drunkard's pulpit. Very hungry, weak, and
bowed down with shame, he began to think
that Heaven had willed his death. The
darkest hour of his life seemed at hand when
he heard a voice in the square below him,
and opening his eyes quickly, beheld no

"HE WAS LEFT ALONE IN THAT DRUNKARD'S PULPIT."

other than Barbarino, the clown, and with him his pretty daughter, Nina.

To Scavezzo, the sight was as a vision from Heaven.

"Oh, glory to God this night!" he cried piteously; "here, at last, are those who know me."

Old Barbarino pretended to hear the voice and to be amazed at the sound of it.

"Hark!" cried he, standing suddenly before the pillory; "I could have sworn that I heard the voice of his Excellency, Scavezzo, at whose word we are to be banished from Venice to-day. Yet when I look up, I see a common rogue standing in the pillory as any drunkard of the city."

He made as though to pass on; but the trembling Canon implored him with tears in his eyes.

"For the love of God, one moment!" he wailed; "I am not what I appear to be, — I am Scavezzo; oh, Heaven help me! I speak the truth to you. Yesterday, I was your enemy; to-day I will be your friend. I swear it on the Cross, — I ask it on my knees — "

Old Barbarino seemed to hesitate, but little Nina said, —

"How can he be Scavezzo, father; and if

he is, why should we help him, since there is
a new Canon called Scavezzo across yonder,
and he will not take our home from us?"

"A new Canon," roared Scavezzo, "another
in my place—oh, devils all, you tell me that?"

"Ay, indeed," answered old Barbarino.
"Scavezzo, the Canon, is over there all right,
as every woman in Venice, who heard him
preach this morning, will swear."

Scavezzo listened no more. He opened
his lips — no sound came out. His head
drooped forward. He had fainted.

IV

At noon next day in his own house, whither
the clowns carried him, they told Scavezzo
the story of the jest.

"Ah," said Giacomo, his servant, "nothing
but a pilgrimage to Rome will blot this out,
my master. To think of it, that they should
dress up this wood-carver with their powders
and their paints until, had he stepped into
your pulpit, your own mother would not have
discovered him."

"But he did not step into my pulpit,
Giacomo — oh, tell me that he did not!"

Giacomo's eyes twinkled.

"You must ask Frà Giovanni about that," he said; "perchance old Barbarino has a bad memory, Excellency, — a clown's way of speaking, you understand, which implied, as I live, that you should preach to clowns."

Scavezzo sighed.

"It is a long way to Rome, Giacomo," he expostulated, " nevertheless — "

"Nevertheless, Venice has a longer memory, my master. The city loves her clowns, — ay, better than any Canon that ever wore the purple."

Scavezzo shook his head sadly.

" Ay," he said, "that is a lesson I do not need to learn, Giacomo."

A MIRACLE OF BELLS

I

LAY-BROTHER NICOLO watched the last of the beggars quit the aisles of the great church, and then bestirred himself to close it for the night. One by one he put out the tapers, which still cast their wan light upon the marble pavements. East and west he went to lock the gates of the porches. Silently and swiftly he drew the heavy leathern curtains which shut his brethren, the Servite fathers, from the merry life of the world upon the waters ; swiftly, too, he covered the altars, and carried the great golden crucifix to the sacristy. For supper, hot and savoury and steaming, was already filling the refectory with delicious odours, and lay-brother Nicolo was very hungry.

One last look round, a moment's pause to light the lantern which showed him the way to the door of the sacristy, completed his uncongenial task. Clear as his conscience was, he did not wish to linger in the darkened

church when the people had left it and the
outer gate was closed. By and by he would
live with the saints; but until that day came
he preferred the chatter of his brethren in
refectory and in cloister.

And there were such queer sights and
sounds in that lonely fane when all the tapers
were out and the dim red lamps cast shadows
before the altars, and the very effigies of
dead martyrs seemed reanimated and living.

On this particular evening of March old
Nicolo could have sworn that he heard a
sound, as of the pattering of little feet, at
the very moment when he was about to close
the last of the doors and to hurry to the
odorous stew awaiting him. Truth to tell,
he held his lantern high, and listened intently
while some seconds passed; but the sound
was not repeated, and, eager to be reassured,
the trembling monk turned the heavy key in
the lock and fled that holy place of spirits
and of shadows.

"What a thing to imagine!" he said to
himself, as he crossed the cloister and drew
his hood about his ears, for the wind blew
cold upon Venice from the mountains.
"Surely I am growing old and will be the
better for a cup of wine. A child at night-

fall in the church of the Servites! As well seek an honest man in the booths of Rialto."

Now, this surmise was well enough in an ordinary way, but it chanced to be ill chosen on that memorable evening. Indeed, at the very moment when the good friar laughed at his delusions, and helped himself plentifully to the savoury dish, little Nina, the daughter of old Barbarino, the clown, was smiling through her tears in the church he had left.

She told herself that there, at any rate, none would molest her until day came. She it was who had watched the lay-brother as he put out those tapers one by one; she who had prayed to all the saints and angels that she might lie the night in the warm church, and that none might discover her. No home was hers in all that glittering city of waters; no hand stretched out to give her aught but blows. Her father, Barbarino, the fool, begrudged her the very shelter of the booth he clowned in, — over there on the Piazza by the great church of St. Mark.

She had no memory nor name of the mother whose child she was. Nina, the people called her as she capered in the dress of Columbine, — Nina, the fairy; Nina of the black eyes; Nina, the dancing girl.

She would repeat the words to herself, as she lay, hungry and alone, in whatever shelter the unbefriending night might give her; she would ask if the years to come had nothing but such empty praise for her reward. She had lived through sixteen summers; yet a summer of life was unknown to her. Nina of the black eyes, the people said, for the people did not see the tears upon the cheek nor know the loneliness in the heart of the child.

Frà Nicolo closed the church, and Nina dried up her tears. She had no fear of the shadows. The twinkling lamps before the altars were for her lanterns to guide the feet of angels. In the darkness the Christ came down to her from the Cross; the saints from the pictures. Or she would love to tell herself that this great building was a palace of which she was the mistress.

She would people it in her imagination with the nobles of Venice; with princes in habits of silver; with fair women, whose jewels shone as the jewels upon the altar of the Virgin; with young girls, whose beauty her own should surpass. Music she heard in fancy and the words of lovers; but always the words of one whose image was before her day and night, Christoforo, Count of Carmagnola, that reckless lord of the city, whose wealth was the envy of Venice, whose beauty was her admiration.

Little Nina had touched his cloak once as he passed to his gondola from the Palace. His image had been with her sleeping or waking since that day; there was a world of happiness in the foolish dreams which brought him to her side. She told herself, girlishly, that she would love him to her life's end, though never might she speak to him nor hear his voice.

Nina slept a young girl's sleep; a sleep of sweet dreams and of troubles forgotten. Cold as the great church was, nevertheless she could rest therein and forget the booth where her father clowned to please the people, and she was beaten when the money bag was empty. Usually, her dreams would last until day came and old Frà Nicolo lit the candles for the first Mass; but on this night of March, in the year 1701, the voice of the storm and the moaning of the wind broke in upon her slumbers so that eleven o'clock had hardly been struck by the great

72

bell above her head when she opened her
eyes and began to ask herself where she was.
For the first time in all her life a terrible
fear of the darkness took possession of her.
She started to her feet, with her dreams still
clinging to her eyes, and peered into the
shadows of the church. A sense of loneliness
and of dread, in no way to be explained,
made her limbs tremble. She fell upon her
knees before the great altar, and prayed as
she had never prayed before.

" Lord God, I know that I am not alone."

The strange prayer was as a salve to her
fears. She rose up from the steps of the
altar, and began to laugh at herself.

" Who is there that would harm the clown's
daughter?" she asked herself. " Who is
there that would come to the church of the
Servites when Venice sleeps? Olà, I am a
ninny to be frightened by my dreams."

The argument was good, but not altogether
satisfying. It suggested, after all, that some
other outcast might have done as she had
done, and found a sanctuary from the bitter
wind in the aisles of the Servite church.
The mere contemplation of such a possibility
quickened her heart and muted her tongue.
She stood listening intently for any strange

sound in the building. She feared to raise a hand, almost to breathe. Yet no sound, such as she listened for, was to be heard. Only the wind sighing beneath the eaves; only the waters lapping the marble steps before the porch of the monastery.

She said, for the second time, that she was a baby to think of such things; and so returned to the dark chapel, and tried to sleep once more. The visions began to come again, the dreams to weave the smiles about her lips, when a sound within the church once more brought her to her feet and sent the blood rushing to her head. It was the sound of a key grating in the lock of the sacristy door.

Nina started to her feet and ran from the chapel to the great nave of the church. She was not quite sure yet that she had not dreamed the thing. She began to argue with herself again, asking who would come to the monastery when Venice slept. A repetition of the sound froze the argument upon her lips. No longer was there any opportunity to doubt.

She heard the door of the sacristy creak upon its hinges. She heard the whisper of voices, the muted tread of men who crossed the marble pavement of the ambulatory, and were coming to the nave of the church. She knew that she was no longer alone, and, stricken by a terror which surpassed any terror she had imagined, she ran back to the chapel and lay, all huddled up and shivering, in the shadow of the oaken screen that divided the transept from the church.

"Who is it? Who can come at such an hour?" she asked herself helplessly, and bewildered. The idea that the monks themselves had heard of her hiding-place, and were there to punish her, was her first thought; but it ceased to help her when she remembered that they would not come in darkness with muted steps. And if not the monks, who then? She dared not to think out an answer to her own question.

Child that she was, she had heard of those dangers of plot and counterplot, which then threatened her own city and the prince of her own city. She had heard of men who were awake to conspiracies when others slept; who hid themselves in the vaults and the cellars by night, yet were the ornaments of Venice by day.

Instinctively she guessed that such men as these had invaded her hiding-place. They had obtained possession of the keys of the church, she thought, and were there to speak of things which, whispered even in the shadows outside, might set the heads of those who whispered them between the pillars of St. Mark. And if her guess was right, what hope or chance of life had she? They would kill her, she said, kill her and cast her body into the lagoon. Her crime would be that she had seen their faces, had known their meeting-place.

This affrighting thought sent her back still farther into the great patch of shadow which the screen cast upon the pavement of the chapel. She feared even that the men would hear the beating of her heart. The creak of the sacristy door as it shut gently upon its hinges was like ice upon her limbs. She counted the muted footsteps, and saw that they were very near to her. She could distinguish the whisper of voices and hear the question of one and the answer of another.

The men were searching the church, then, they would find her presently, they would drag her out, they would — but she had not the courage to imagine more, and a heavy sob broke from her, though she knew that discovery was but a little removed from death. Then she heard the sound of voices.

" Is it you, Count? "

" It is I, Orso."

" You heard nothing? "

" I heard the wind under the eaves."

" Is Paolo there? "

" He is at my side."

" Then it was not he — holy God, what a thought ! "

" You said, Orso? "

" That I heard a sound as of someone sobbing."

" Pah! it was the wine you drank. Thrust your sword in that confessional, and then tell me who sobs."

Nina heard the man obey. She could picture him thrusting his shining blade into the dark recesses about the pillars of the nave. He would come, by and by, to the chapel where she lay, and that sword would tell her story.

" Well, do you find anything? "

" Dust — I find that, Count, and the books of the priest. Saint John, what a fright I had! "

The man thus called Count laughed softly.

"Who would be in the church of the Servites at this hour?" he asked.

"The police, perhaps; they are everywhere."

The other made a gesture of impatience.

"It is time to end this nonsense," said he. "Uncover your lantern, and let us see what that can show us. Paolo will stand at the door of the sacristy meanwhile. If there is any friar out of bed at this hour, we shall know how to talk to him. And I will trouble you to take off my shoes, my friend; they groan like a sick man!"

With these words, the men left their place by the pulpit, and began to walk very silently and quickly towards the great western door. Nina counted their footsteps, and as the sounds died away, she took courage, and peered over the low screen of the chapel wherein she had slept. There was moonlight at this time, for the wind had lifted the low clouds of evening, and the painted windows took shape again, showing glorious visions of saints and angels.

The child could see two of the men quite clearly as they passed in and out of the side chapels; but the apparition was fitful, for the shadows were deep and many, and she was too fearful to leave her hiding-place for long. Rather, she drew back into the darkness again, and prayed with all her heart that someone would come to the church.

"They will kill me," she thought, "and no one will know. I shall never see the stars again." The footsteps were very near just then. She could hear the low voices of the men again.

"Where are your friars now, my friend?"

"There is yet the chapel, Count."

"Ha! You have the knees of a woman. Cast a light again."

Nina was crouching then almost under the bench built into the screen. Though her face was hidden in her ragged black cloak, nevertheless she saw the flashing rays of the lantern, and expected every moment that a hand would touch her shoulder. She did not know that her rags, black and sombre, matched the shadows so well that even the lantern did not betray her. When, at last, she heard the receding footsteps, and began to believe that she was undiscovered, it seemed to her that a miracle had been wrought. God had saved her, then — and for what? The answer came as some voice of the night. That she, in her turn, might save Venice.

The voice made her tremble, but it was no longer with an emotion of fear. Her naturally quick brain, trained to readiness by her vagrant life, grasped in an instant the truth of that which she saw. These men, what were they doing in the church of the Servites, why did they speak in whispers, why did they bare their feet? There could be but one reason, — they were the enemies of Venice.

Nina had heard the strange tales then told in the city, of discontent among the nobles, of an appointed day when there would be a new Doge and a new Venice. She had heard that there were spies everywhere, that every man was watched, that no man was discovered. What the police had been unable to do, she, the child, had done, — she had tracked the enemies of the city to their hiding-place. The assurance thrilled her as with a thrill of new pleasure. She, Nina, the waif, must save Venice.

All fear for herself was gone now. Quickly she drew off her torn shoes and stood up, forgetting the cold of the flags and the bare feet which trod them. She must alarm the monastery, she said to herself. She remembered that the police were accustomed to guard the narrow water-way by which the church stood. Their boats, perchance, would even at that moment be near the bridge which the men must cross when their strange work was done. If she could but whisper a word which would bring the police to her side!

Shivering with the cold, nevertheless with brain burning, she crept a little way from her hiding-place. The three men, masked, and wearing black cloaks of prodigious length, stood at that moment in a little chapel on the opposite side of the nave. Taking courage of the fact that the chapel had no windows, they had kindled the tapers set before a picture of St. Augustine, and were kneeling there in an effort, as the girl saw, to raise a great slab of marble which covered one of the altar tombs. When they had lifted it, they took a parchment from the tomb and began to scrutinize it closely, one of them holding up a taper that they might decipher the writing more readily.

Nina said to herself, as she watched them, that this must be the instant of her flight. Swiftly, as a shadow in the moonlight, she darted across the nave and sought a new hiding-place in the ambulatory. Panting for breath, with hands pressed upon her beating heart, she listened as a deer that is hunted. But the men were still absorbed in the paper. She could see that one of them held an ink-horn, and that another was writing. She took courage and ran on to the door of the sacristy. The moment of deliverance was at hand.

The door had been closed, but the key was still in the lock. The girl's hand was already upon the door when she remembered that its creaking, when the others opened it, had awakened her earlier in the night. She perceived that it would not be possible again to turn the key without discovery. The danger was one she had not anticipated. She knew that the moments were precious, as never moments had been in all her life. She must save Venice, — she, Nina, the daughter of Barbarino, the clown, They would kill her if they knew — and yet she must save Venice.

Hours seemed to pass while she stood trembling at the door in a fear of indecision and of anxiety. Once, the man who held the inkhorn for the other to write, let the scabbard of his sword jar upon the marble pavement, and she started back at the sound

"THEY TOOK A PARCHMENT FROM THE TOMB AND BEGAN TO
SCRUTINIZE IT CLOSELY."

and could scarcely forbear to cry out. For
quite a long time after that, she leant against
a pillar of the chancel, afraid to raise a hand,
or even to turn her head.

When her courage came, and she made a
movement as though to reach the door again,
the miracle of the night happened. A bell,
the sanctus bell above the chancel arch, rang
out clearly in the silence — one sweet, linger-
ing note which echoed over the sleeping
waters, and brought the three men to their
feet as at the voice of a judgment of
Heaven.

" Ha! — do you hear that, Count?"

" Have I no ears? Put out the light."

" You have the paper, Count?"

" I have my sword. To the door, and
every man for himself."

Nina heard the threat, but cared not at all
now. She had found a way. Crouching
against the pillar of the chancel, she had
trodden unwittingly upon the rope of the
sanctus bell, and thus alarmed the monastery.
And, once the way was shown to her, she
followed it readily. Falling upon her knees,
for she thought that death was very near to
her, she took the rope in her hands, and
clanged the bell incessantly. The noise of it

was no longer that of a note sweet and
sonorous. It jarred upon the ear as a dirge.
It brought lights to the windows of the
neighbouring houses. Men cried out to men
that the church was on fire. Other bells
began to ring, — above all, the voices of the
guard were heard. Venice was saved, she
said. The work was for others now. The
men would kill her, but Venice would
remember.

There was a great noise outside the church
at this time; the patter of steps, the flash of
lanterns, cries, and answering cries. The
three men stood all together in a great circle
of moonlight cast upon the pavement of the
nave. Their swords were drawn, they turned
about and again about as though the danger
lurked in every shadow. But their irresolution was not enduring. Two of them, stricken
by terror of the unseen, ran boldly to the
sacristy door and passed through it. The
third followed with slower steps; and when
he came to the chancel arch, he stood an
instant with the moonbeams falling full upon
his face.

Nina, who saw him thus for the first time,
knew in that moment why they had called
him Count. She looked upon the lord of

Carmagnola himself, — upon him of whom she had dreamed through many a weary night of cold and hunger. Her lover, as she, the dancing girl, had called him, stood before her, — on the threshold of death, she said. And she had killed him! In five minutes, in ten, the police would come! Anguish beyond any of fear or of physical suffering almost stilled her heart. She knelt upon the pavement, and no longer were her tears held back.

The man heard her cry and strode to the place where she lay with the moonlight giving golden threads to her hair. He thought that he had found the spy who betrayed him. He drew his dagger, telling himself that one other at least should die that night. But when the white beams showed him a young girl's face looking up pitifully into his own, he thrust the weapon in its sheath again, and stood regarding her with silent astonishment.

"Child," he asked sternly, "who are you, and why are you here?"

"I am Nina, the daughter of Barbarino," she said, between her sobs.

"What does Nina, the daughter of Barbarino, do alone in a church at midnight?"

"Oh, Excellency, the cold and the hunger drove me —"

"A beggar's tale," was his answer as he stooped and seized her by the hands, dragging her out that the soft light might show him her face clearly. "Who sent you to this place?"

She thought that he was about to kill her, and she cringed before the blow she feared.

"God sent me," she answered at last, "to save Venice."

He laughed scornfully.

"What did they pay you, girl? Tell the truth — do you hear? Whose servant are you?"

"The servant of poverty, Excellency, — the servant of hunger. Oh, believe me, I have not eaten bread since yesterday at dawn. And I came here because the wind is bitter, and my feet are bare. Then I saw the light, and I heard your voice. God help me! I did not know that it was you."

She buried her face in her hands while the Count of Carmagnola stood regarding her with a new amazement. He had hardly seen a more beautiful face in all Venice. The girl, he thought, was like one of the children in the picture above the high altar. He

"SHE CRINGED BEFORE THE BLOW SHE FEARED."

asked himself how he could have lived in the city for three years, and have passed her by. And a pretty face could always win upon his generosity.

"Come," he said, as if in an inspiration, "you say that you did not know. Prove your words to me. The police are at the gate, as you hear. Show me a door by which I may escape them, and I will believe your story."

The appeal awakened her from the trance of fear and grief. All her love for Venice was forgotten in a moment. She would save the man her dreams had given to her for a lover. Yet how? She could hear the cries without; she could see the flash of lanterns; she knew that the police would come to the church before many minutes had passed; she feared that all the gates were already watched. What hope was there, then?

"Lord Count," she cried in the second inspiration of the night, "there was a way, but I know not if it be a way still. Yet, if you will follow — "

She stood up and faced him. He listened and heard voices in the sacristy; he could see the flickering rays of a lantern; he knew that the police were at the very gates.

"Child," he said very quietly, "show me your way, for it is the only one."

Nina waited for no other command, but stretched out her hand and thrust it into that of the man.

"Come, Excellency," she said eagerly, "the door is behind the great organ."

With this she crossed the nave and mounted the winding staircase by which the organ loft was reached. She remembered that her nights in the church had shown to her a wicket-gate in the wall behind the organ, and once she had unbarred that gate and passed out, to find herself upon the leads of the monastery. From these she had gone on until she came to an old stone staircase, at the foot of which flowed one of the narrowest water-ways in all Venice. That staircase should save the man's life, she said.

"The door is here, Excellency. Let your hands feel for the bolt; we are safe if we can but lift it."

The man stopped to reckon with his chances no more. One backward glance showed him the floor of the church below,— the dancing lanterns and the figures of those who held them. He unbarred the door swiftly, and followed the girl through it to the broad leads of the monastery. Venice lay beneath ; Venice awakened. The bells of many churches were ringing. A panic of night become day had begun to seize upon the city. The fugitives could see the boats of the police at the steps of the southern porch. A great crowd had gathered from all the neighbouring houses ; men shouted to men that an enemy was in the palace, and that the Doge was killed. Women stood at the windows of the lighted houses.

Carmagnola watched the scene while he could have counted ten. For the first time he began to believe in the possibility of ulti-mate escape. This waif of Venice with the black eyes and the little soft hand ; this dancing girl, who had stumbled so fatefully upon the nest of his schemes, would enable him, after all, to pursue these schemes.

That the others had been taken he did not believe. And if they had, with what could the police charge them ? This child, who now held his hand so timidly, would not betray him. He read her face truly. She was not the first woman in Venice who had trembled at his touch. A kiss upon her lips, he argued, would silence her for ever. There was no other that he feared or thought of in all the city.

"Your way is a good one, little Nina," he said lightly, turning from the scene about the church door to her who had saved him; "we will cheat them yet. Show me your staircase, and I will say that I have no better friend in all the city."

Her face flushed with pride and pleasure. The touch of his hand had made her heart leap. She walked as one in sleep, — she, Nina, the dancing girl, side by side with him of whom she had dreamed through many a long night of hunger and of cold.

"My lord," she said, "I am not worthy to be your friend. Here is the water, and my work is done."

She had brought him, as she promised, to the bank of a little canal which wound its dark way amid gaunt and gloomy houses and the homes of the poor. Here the silence of the night was unbroken, — no sound but that of bells ringing musically in the distance came to them over the lapping waters. The Count told himself that the peril was passed. To-morrow would find him in his own house again.

"My little guide," he said, standing a

moment irresolute as at the parting of the ways, "where shall I look at dawn for Nina, the daughter of Barbarino, the clown?"

The question tempted her; but her wits were keener than his in that hour of peril.

"Excellency," she said, drawing back, "you will not look for me in Venice. God forbid — have you forgotten the paper?"

A cry burst from his lips; he caught her by the wrist almost fiercely.

"The paper — what do you know of that; why do you speak of it?"

"Because those who now read it will not be your friends, my lord."

Carmagnola loosed her hands. She could see the diamond button, which clasped the lace about his throat, rise and fall quickly with his heavy breathing. The house of cards he had built was scattered by her words as by a great wind. The paper — the parchment which could send a hundred in Venice to the scaffold, — in whose hands was that now?

"Great God!" he cried aloud; "it lies upon the altar tomb."

Nina drew back trembling before his anger.

"My lord," she stammered, "the others —"

He stopped her with a bitter laugh.

"The others — the others! Paolo, the fool, and Orso, the woman — what have I to do with them, when to-morrow there will be no house in Venice so large that I may find a home in it, no cellar so dark that it will hide me."

She took courage of his distress.

"Lord Count," she pleaded, "there is one who could yet save you from your enemies."

He answered her with a sneer.

"A new Christ — here in Venice, child. One who works miracles?"

"I speak of a priest, my lord."

"Of a priest?"

"Of Frà Giovanni, — of him they call the soldier monk."

He looked at her and ceased to laugh.

"Take me to your priest," he said.

II

It wanted an hour to dawn on the second day of March, in the year 1703, when little Nina, followed quickly by the Count of Carmagnola, stepped from a gondola which had

carried them from Rialto to the island of the
Jews, and rang at the great bell before Frà
Giovanni's gloomy palace.

"Frà Giovanni will save you, my lord,"
she had said again and again during those
anxious moments of flight; "there is none
so powerful as he. I shall ask him and he
will help you. He is my friend."

Carmagnola listened to her indifferently.
He had no coherent thought. The work he
had planned so diligently for weary months,
the house of conspiracy he had built so
laboriously, had been cast down, not by
Doge or Senate, or by any spy — but by
this dancing girl, sent, God knew whence, to
the church of the Servites to save the city
and its people. Never was there a destiny
so ironic. He could have laughed aloud to
think that he and those with him had turned
like frightened women from the voice of
a child. And yet, he said, that child had
sent a hundred brave men to the scaffold.
His own life — what would it be worth to
him henceforth? At dawn every gate must
be shut against him; every cellar would be
searched. What house would harbour him
— what hand befriend him?

"Your priest lives here, little Nina?" he

asked, as she rang the bell, and stood shivering with the cold of morning.

"He is coming now, Excellency; I hear his footsteps. He will listen to me, because he is my friend."

Carmagnola shrugged his shoulders. It was grotesque, he said to himself, that he should have followed this dancing girl at all. The homage that she paid to her friar galled his pride.

"Pah!" he said; "what can a friar do when the police are not your friends? Nevertheless —"

She would have answered him, but the door of the palace opened as he spoke, and the friar himself stood before them. He held a taper in his hand; his capuce was drawn about his ears. The meagre face, seen in that wan light, was such a face as the old painters gave to their saints. The keen, black eyes seemed to cut with their glance. Neither pity nor love could be read in the deep lines of that strange countenance.

"What does the lord of Carmagnola seek of me?" he asked, holding the taper up that the light might fall on the other's face.

Carmagnola suppressed an exclamation.

His name, then, despite his mask, was known to the other.

"I seek sanctuary," he said curtly.

Nina knelt upon the flags and took the friar's hand.

"Father," she cried, "you are my friend; you will save the Lord Count from his enemies."

The priest answered her sternly.

"What have you to do with such things?" he asked.

She had no word for him, but continued to kneel at his feet. When he had looked at them both again, he turned to the Count.

"I will save you from Venice," he said in a low voice. "Enter."

"And this child?"

"Let her go to her home."

"But she has saved my life.'

"Venice will reward her."

Carmagnola hesitated during a moment of irresolution. Then, with deft fingers, he unclasped the great brooch of diamonds from his pourpoint, and pinned it upon the ragged cloak of the kneeling girl.

"Little Nina," he said, as he bent and kissed her, "I shall remember."

The priest, who watched the scene with some contempt, did not hide his impatience.

" Signorè," he exclaimed, " the night grows old, and at dawn — "

He turned and entered the house with Carmagnola at his heels. In a great bare room upon the first floor he lit a second taper and set it on a bureau. Then he finished the sentence he had begun on the steps without.

" At dawn, my lord, Venice will reckon with her enemies."

Carmagnola laughed.

" What does a priest know of the enemies of Venice ? "

" If he should know their names ? "

" The name of one — ? "

" Of all, signorè."

The friar stood like an avenging figure, holding the taper in his hand, and searching the other's face with eyes of steel.

" Of all, signorè," he repeated, in a voice which struck terror to him who heard it.

Carmagnola put up a hand, upon which many jewels glistened, to the clasp of his toga. His cloak was loosed to show a dress of crimson velvet beneath, and the long stola, the emblem of his nobility. He breathed quickly as a baited animal in a moment of respite.

"I am come to the house of a spy, then!" he cried fiercely.

"Say rather to the house of one sent for the salvation of this city, as he was sent ten years ago to save Florence from you and your dupes, my lord."

The Count took a step forward and peered into the face of the other.

"In God's name, who are you?" he asked.

"I am he whom they call the soldier monk," replied the priest, quietly, "and I was in the church of the Servites two hours ago."

"You — in the church!"

The priest did not not notice the interruption.

"I was in the church, signorè. Shall I tell you the names of those who were there with me? Shall I tell you that one of them, a man walking blindly in his own conceit, thinking that he and his unhappy creatures can prevail above the good of Venice, wrote down the names of those creatures upon a parchment? Shall I show you that parchment, my lord — it is here in my breast, for I picked it up when it fell from your hands? Shall I tell you that to-day at dawn the

Councillors will read it as I have read it? Is that what you have come here to learn, — you whom they call the lord of Carmagnola?"

Carmagnola reeled back before the damning accusation.

"Who are you, in God's name?" he asked again.

The priest held up the taper and loosed his friar's habit.

"Look at me again, Lord Count," he whispered.

The Count recovered himself, and peered into the face so close to his own.

" I do not know you," he stammered.

" Again, again, Lord Count — the swordsman of Iseo; you have forgotten him who gave you your life, and is here to-night to give it you again."

He stood awaiting his answer; but Carmagnola's memory had gone back ten years to a day when in a garden of Florence he had stood face to face with the first swordsman in all Italy, and, his weapon being struck from his hand, that swordsman had given him his life.

" I know you," he cried at last in a hoarse voice; " you are the Prince of Iseo."

" As you say, the Prince of Iseo."

" And once more you offer me my life ? "

" It is the reward of her who would have saved Venice to-night."

" There are conditions, of course ? "

The priest smiled.

" When Venice forgives, there are always conditions, Lord Count."

" And you are able to speak in the name of Venice."

" I am able to speak in the name of Venice."

" Then what do you ask of me? "

The priest raised his hand and pointed to the jewels upon the breast of the other.

" That you strip those jewels from you, and give them to the poor; that you leave Venice at dawn and never look upon her spires again; that neither you nor your children's children shall dwell in the house you have built; that Italy shall know you no more, — that as a beggar you shall go out, and as a beggar you shall live. Those are the conditions, Lord Count."

Carmagnola heard him as one who hears sentence of death.

" And if I do not accept them ? "

The priest answered him by leading him to the balcony of the house, and pointing across the water to the great Piazza of St. Mark.

Dawn was breaking, and the domes of the church were already capped with the golden light of the new day.

"Look yonder, my lord," he said grimly; "listen to those cries. They are the shouts of the people, who tell each other that two of the enemies of Venice are enemies no more."

The Count trembled.

"You mean —"

"That the two who were with you in the church of the Servites last night hang head downwards between the columns of the Piazza."

Carmagnola staggered back into the room.

"I will save the honour of my name," he cried.

.   .   .   .   .

There was a great procession around the Piazza of St. Mark after sundown that day. The bells of the city rang joyously; bright fires were lit on all the open places; candles were set in the windows of every house. In the great church itself the priests sang a Te Deum, and countless lights burned before the altars, and thanksgiving was offered for the safety of Venice and the death of her enemies. Outside in the square a vast throng swarmed about one whom stalwart arms held up, about a dancing girl whom they had crowned with flowers and carried, as often they carried images, high above the people on a golden throne.

" Viva Nina, the daughter of Barbarino ! "

" Viva ! Viva ! the Queen of Venice ! "

" She has saved our city. A miracle of the bells was sent. Viva ! Viva ! "

But little Nina, thus snatched in a moment from want and penury and cold and hunger, did not heed the cries nor the gifts which were poured upon her.

" She weeps," a woman said.

" It is for joy," they answered her.

But one in Venice knew that she wept for the man.

She had saved him as she promised ; but she would see him no more.

"THE WOLF OF CISMON"

I

LEOPARDI, the bandit, was to die. Venice heard the news incredulously, on the second day of March, in the year 1704. Throughout the city no other name was on the people's lips. "He dies at sunset." The very gondoliers took up the cry and repeated it mockingly, as they sent their black boats merrily across the dancing waters of the lagoon. Men gathered together near the Ducal Palace and discussed the story in muted whispers. Women stopped their gondolas beneath the Bridge of Sighs, and showed each other, morbidly, the wall of the dungeon behind which "The Wolf of Cismon" lay. For Leopardi had been the handsomest, the most daring bandit that ever ruled the mountains above Vicenza.

Leopardi was to die. Men shook their heads doubtingly; the more knowing among them scoffed openly at the news.

"He has ten lives, comrades; I will believe your story when I see his body. There is no rope in Italy which will strangle Leopardi of Cismon. Besides, has not the great friar promised him — ?"

"Pah, what can our Father Giovanni do when the Three have willed it? They say that Leopardi is to die at sunset, and his body is to be cast into the lagoon. The friar interceded for him, but he was not listened to, my friends. It is a black day for him to take a second place in the Council."

A girl, who had overheard the boatmen's talk, chimed in with her defending word.

"Believe it not," she said; "let Mocenigo, who condemned him, look to himself. I would sooner wear the shoes of Leopardi of the mountains than the golden slippers of the Pope. God send such a man to the altar with me."

She spoke as though "The Wolf of Cismon" had been her own lover; and many a woman in Venice uttered a secret prayer that day for the robber upon whom the iron hand of justice at length had fallen. For ten years Leopardi had been the terror of the mountain towns from Iseo to Mestre.

THE SIGNORS OF THE NIGHT

In all her lists of bandits, Italy had never known one bolder or more beloved by the common people.

"The Wolf of Cismon" they called him in the mountains. "The Devil of the Hills" was the title the police of Venice gave to him. And these police had him caged at last in the dungeons of the Ducal Palace. He had sworn a rash oath that he would steal the gold chain from the neck of Mocenigo, the judge, and he had kept his word. But he had forgotten to reckon with the police.

They arrested him at the house of one of his kinsmen in Torcello, and promised him a short shrift. By some means, none knew how, he had earned the friendship of the priest, Giovanni, who had interceded with the Council for him. But Venice could not pardon a rogue who had robbed one of her senators; and the decree went out that he was to be strangled by the executioner, and his body to be cast into the lagoon. In spite of this, there were plenty in the city to declare that Leopardi would cheat the executioner even yet — aye, would cheat the very devil with a rope in his hand.

"We will believe it when he is dead," they cried.

But others said, —

"He is to die at sunset."

II

LEOPARDI, the bandit, was sleeping on his bed of straw when Pietro, the gaoler, awoke him. They said in the prison that he had done little but sleep and eat since the Supreme Court condemned him. In his waking hours he sang the strophes of Tasso, or amused his captors with wondrous stories of the great women who had been his patrons — of the villages he had raided, and the treasure he had stored up. A merrier prisoner had never been caged in the dungeons of the palace.

His tuneful voice could quicken his gaolers' steps as they went down to the cells, or up again to the blessed light of day. His laughter was infectious, and not to be resisted. The very guards learnt to love him, and to smuggle in the presents which his friends in the city carried every day to the door of the prison. "A pity, indeed, that such as he must die," was the saying in every mouth.

Pietro, the gaoler, touched his prisoner upon the shoulder, and Leopardi sat up at once. He still wore the suit of grey velvet in which they had arrested him ; and his magnificent black cloak, with the trimming of bear-skin, served well for a blanket. Though there was but the pitiful light of a lantern in the cell, it could not hide altogether the superb figure and the pleasing face of the bandit.

There were few handsomer men in all Italy, as the people said ; few with such well-shaped limbs, or such a fine carriage, or such irresistible, merry eyes. Peril had not warred with that figure, nor danger put out the light of jest which had showed the ruler of the mountains so good a way to riches and to victory. Standing, as it seemed, on the very threshold of death, he could yet greet as a friend the very man who came to tell him that the end was at hand.

" Behold ! it is thou, Pietro. There is news, then."

Pietro hung his head.

" There is very bad news, my friend."

Leopardi rubbed his eyes as though the

garish light troubled them ; then he dusted the straw from his fine clothes.

" Body of a Canon ! " he cried. " I am devoured, Pietro — devoured ! You hear that ! Then tell his Excellency, your master, that if he would not shake himself here every morning — "

Pietro raised his hands as though against a blasphemy.

" Hush, hush ! " he said. " You are speaking of the Serene Prince, Leopardi."

Leopardi laughed lightly.

" The news, the news — what of the news, Pietro ? " he exclaimed, as he adjusted the dirty lace about his throat, and felt for the sword which should have been at his side.

Pietro hung his head again.

" The priest is here," he said humbly.

" How, the priest ? "

" As I say. He comes to tell you that it is to-day."

" To-day ! What is to-day ? Would you have it to-morrow, Pietro ? "

" Do not jest, I beg of you, comrade. The priest who comes will tell you of the day."

Leopardi looked at the gaoler in a dazed way for a moment. Then he laughed until the cell rang again.

" Ho, ho ! " he said; " it needs a priest for that. There is no one else in Venice with the courage. Saint John ! When your Doge comes to Cismon, Pietro, I will show him a like courtesy. I will send him a Bishop to say that he shall hang at dawn."

Pietro shrugged his shoulders.

" Ah ! " he exclaimed. " When that day comes, Leopardi, there will be horses on the Canallazzo."

The bandit slapped him on the back with a great hand which shook every bone in old Pietro's body.

" Barrel of Bacchus ! " said he ; " what news I shall have for your ear when the sun sets again, Pietro ! Bring in your priest. I would prefer a flask of Armagnac, but, since your master plays the host so scurvily, we will even be content with this flask of divinity — which, I 'll wager, shall be as dry as the lips of a councillor's wife. The priest, the priest, Pietro ! Am I a heretic that you delay so ? "

He thrust the other from the cell, and stood for a moment with his hands twitching curiously, and a drooping of the curves of the mouth, which spoke of nerves at high tension and of effort to conceal the emotion he felt. But when, presently, an old friar came shuffling into the place, the smile was on his face again, the laughter in his eyes.

"Your blessing, brother," he asked, dropping on his knee with an air of great humility.

The priest raised his fingers and blessed him.

"My son," he said, "open your heart to me, for you are to die in an hour."

Leopardi sighed, but did not rise from his knees.

"Oh," he exclaimed, "God give me a good memory, for there is much on my soul, brother."

The friar seated himself upon the wooden stool, the single ornament of the cell, and bent his ear to listen. Leopardi, meanwhile, curled himself up in the straw and began to pick at the ears of it.

"Brother," said he, "yours is a mission of charity. If you would do me a service, the last I shall ever ask of you, I beg you remember that there is one in Cismon dear to me beyond all that have been my friends. I speak of little Beatrice, the daughter of Gianotti, the vintner. You will tell her how I died, brother?"

The priest nodded his head.

"I will not forget her," he said, "yet think rather of your sins, my son, for assuredly —"

Leopardi cut him short.

"It is of my sins I am thinking, brother. Help me to that, I beseech you. There is in the mountain town of Valdagno a young woman whose memory can fill my eyes with tears. I speak of little Marietta, the daughter of Colleoni, the miller."

The priest raised his hands in a gesture of despair.

"Another!" he exclaimed.

"Ay, as you say, brother, there is another. She is Susanna, the daughter of Villani of Lugo. Hasten to her, I beg of you —"

The friar rose from his seat and turned to the door angrily.

"You shall die with the jest upon your lips," he exclaimed sternly. "The church has no word for such as you."

Leopardi made a grimace and ceased to pluck at the straw.

"Ah," he said, "if you would have listened, I would have told you of the twenty men whose throats we cut at Cittadella. Come again to-morrow, brother, and you shall hear of little Elena —"

"To-morrow," said the priest, in a low voice, "to-morrow the police will be looking for your body in the lagoon, my son."

He quitted the cell, covering his ears with his cowl that they might be deaf to such blasphemies. When he was gone, Leopardi stood up and the smile left his face again. The doubt which had troubled him ten minutes ago returned with new intensity. "How if this friar speaks the truth?" he asked himself. Of all those he had known and served in Venice, but one remained to be his friend. He thought of another friar, of the great Frà Giovanni, who had promised that he should not die.

"Saint John!" he said, "the Capuchin has never lied yet. He will save me even now. It will be time enough to ask myself how when the rope is about my neck."

III

THE death that Leopardi was to die was the death of the rope and the trap. They would strangle him in the corridor of the prison, and afterwards cast his body into the lagoon. Such a sentence had been passed upon "The Wolf of Cismon" by Mocenigo, the President of the Criminal Court; and such a sentence the executioner of Venice hastened to carry out so soon as the friar had left the cell of the condemned.

Whatever fear of death troubled Leopardi, at the moment when the gaolers came to him, as they thought for the last time, they found him, as ever, indifferent apparently both to their presence and its meaning. And there was not a single servant of the prison who did not regret the errand, or treasure up a genuine sympathy for this "Devil of the Hills," who had ever been the friend of the poor and the friendless.

"Courage, Leopardi; they will not hurt you. A moment with the rope about your neck, and after that nothing."

So spoke Pietro, the gaoler, as he endeavoured to slip a cord over the hands of the condemned. But Leopardi was too quick for him.

"One moment, good Pietro," cried he. "What! you would truss me like a fowl! Out on you for a scurvy friend! How shall I kiss my hand to the pretty women on the other side of the way if there is a cord upon my wrists?"

Pietro sighed.

"When next you kiss your hand, signorè, it will be in purgatory," said he.

Leopardi pinched his cheek good-humouredly.

"Then I will make a cool place for thee, old Pietro. Come, a cup of wine in charity. Would you send me up yonder with lips of sand? Ho, ho! a thirsty saint would never do. Bring in the wine, rascal, and to the devil with the rest."

The old gaoler shook his head sadly; but he fetched a flask of wine, for this was permitted to the condemned. When the bandit had emptied the cup he professed himself ready.

"Come," he said, "we will go and look at your peep-show, old Pietro."

Pietro flung the door of the cell wide open.

"God have mercy on your soul, Leopardi of Cismon," he said devoutly.

There were half-a-dozen soldiers in the corridor of the prison, and they stood with drawn swords while the condemned passed from his cell. Leopardi, playing his rôle to the last, was singing the old proverb:

"Venetia, Venetia,
Chi non ti vede non ti pretia,"

when he caught sight of them; but he stopped suddenly as he beheld the shining blades; and a quick eye would have seen him stagger against the wall.

"Courage," whispered the gaoler.

"A true word, old Pietro," he said, recovering himself by a great effort; "when last I had the pleasure of seeing these gentlemen in the mountains, it was a word their officer addressed to them. 'Courage,' he said — and he ran, old Pietro. Holy Virgin, how he ran! Give me but the chance, and I will show thee here and now — "

An officer of the guard, appearing suddenly in the corridor, cried "Silence!" and the troop presented arms. The condemned man ceased to jest, for he saw the open trap through which his body was to be cast into the waters. There came in that instant the thought that Frà Giovanni had betrayed him, after all. He was to die, then, he who had been the king of the mountains and the terror of the cities; he, who had known no other master than his own will; whose word had been a terrible law, — this Venice would not spare him. Young in years, the love of his life surged up for a moment and became an agony. He looked round about him wistfully, as though the priest, who had promised to save him, lurked somewhere in the shadows. He was as brave as any in Italy, but this bitterness of death, after he had told himself that he was not to die, was a torture passing words.

" He must come," he said to himself; "he has never been known to lie — he will not desert me."

The hope permitted him to remember his courage, in spite of the place and the scene. And it was a scene grim enough to have affrighted even " The Wolf of Cismon." Death seemed written on every wall, on every face. Light of dim lanterns struck the vaulted ceiling, and shone back from the dark water of the canal without. The soldiers themselves were as figures of stone. The air was hot, and breathed the pestilence of dungeons. When the masked executioner stepped forward and touched the condemned, he started as one aroused from a fitful sleep. The priest had deserted him, he said. There could be no pardon now; no pardon as he stood beneath that rope and looked through the narrow trap-door whereby they would cast out his body presently. He had lived his life. He would never see the mountains again. But, at least, he would die without shame.

"Signorè," said the executioner, as he slipped a cord lightly over the prisoner's ankles and another about his wrists, "I ask your forgiveness."

The robber watched the operation with curious eyes. He stifled the horror which gripped at his heart and remembered that he was Leopardi of Cismon.

"You are forgiven, signorè," he said, with the air of a prince. "Do your work quickly, and my friends shall pay you more money than there is in this cursed city."

"Silence!" cried the Captain of the Guard. "If you have no prayer to say, hold your tongue, rogue."

"My prayer, signorè, is for Venice, that she may always find soldiers who can run like your Excellency."

It was the last word he spoke in the dungeons of the city. Scarcely had it left his lips when the rope tightened about his neck and he was hauled from his feet upward to the roof of the corridor. For long minutes, as it seemed to him, his very heart threatened to burst. Thunderous noises rang in his ears; his eyes showed him a crimson vision of woeful shapes and forms as the blood went leaping to his brain. He struggled madly to touch with his feet any place that should, if it were but for an instant, release the agonising grip of the cord about his throat. Strange voices cried to him as with the greeting of the doomed. He felt himself sinking down, down, to some unfathomed abyss far below the earth. Then there was a rush of water in his ears —

" Was he dead ? " asked the Captain of the Guard, as the body of the robber fell heavily into the dark water of the canal. " You were quick to-night, Gerardo."

The executioner answered evasively.

" When he comes back, Venice will see a miracle, Excellency."

The Captain turned away, glad to leave that place of pestilent odours and of darkness. And through all the city there went the word that Leopardi of Cismon was dead.

IV

THERE was a rush of water in Leopardi's ears, the sensation as of a cascade pouring over his very brain. He opened his eyes and beheld strange green lights flashing before him ; he stretched out his arms, and the half-tied cords fell from them. A mighty effort, instinctive, the effort of one who had been a swimmer since his childhood, brought him to the surface of the canal ; but the half of his senses were yet lacking, and he sank again, deep down to the very mud and slime in the bed of the waters.

It was a terrible struggle, a battle with death waged by one whom the finger of death had touched already. Minutes passed, and still the drowning man knew nothing of that which was happening to him ; nothing of the circumstances which had sent him down there to the darkness of the river's bed. All that he did was done upon an impulse of habit. His agonising struggles to come up again and breathe the cold air of the night were the dictates of his nature crying out for breath.

When he rose to the surface of the water for the second time, nature gained a little strength and began to befriend him. He saw great buildings above him and lights flashing from those buildings. He heard the voices of men and the splash of oars. Reason returned to him; he cried aloud with the joy of life given back, of death defeated.

" Great God! I live, I live," he said; " the priest has saved me, after all; I shall see my home again. Heaven give me strength."

It was all clear to him now, both the plan of his escape and the end of the plan. He knew that the executioner had but half strangled him that he might fight for his life out there in the darkness of the waters. He understood that he must make one supreme effort to cheat Venice and his enemies. He would rule in the mountains again; would live the old life. Frà Giovanni had been his friend. He vowed that he would repay with an offering such as priest had never dreamed of.

It was almost dark at this hour, and the lamps were beginning to shine as stars in the windows of the palaces. Leopardi lay with his head thrown back, washed like a dead thing by the ebbing water. Though a great pain hurt his lung, and noises were still ringing in his brain, he paid no heed to his own condition, but reflected rather on the peril which still hovered about him. For all that he knew, the police might be already seeking his body. He listened for the splash of oars as a deer listens for the dogs.

Far away, the notes of a guitar rang out musically on the night air. Venice was beginning her watch of pleasure. Here and there upon the great Canalazzo a gondola passed, carrying its owner to some *fête* or carnival. Leopardi said that if he could swim to one of those boats and cast himself upon the mercy of the boatman, he would fear his enemies no more. He took courage of the thought, and striking out with a gentle stroke, he gained the shelter of the prison wall and pulled himself hand over hand by it. A splash, he imagined, would betray him. A new executioner would be found — and then!

The stones of the wall were rough to his hands; green slime, revolting and clammy, marked the line of waters. The bandit might have been some vampire creeping away from the prison as he dragged himself toward the open lagoon and the place of safety. Often he paused with a little tremor of fear as he thought that he heard the dip of an oar or the whisper of a voice behind him. Then he would snatch a few yards and cast back his head so that the green waves ran almost to his mouth.

"I will cheat them yet," he muttered, as though in self-encouragement. "When next the Wolf of Cismon barks, let Venice take care of her judges."

Half-an-hour must have passed in this alternation of hope and fear. When, at last, he had crept the whole length of the prison wall and had turned the corner of it, he beheld the great lagoon, the silent sea above which Venice towers. The spectacle was as of some haven of promise to reward him for his hour of suffering. All the courage of his nature, all his reckless contempt of authority and those who stood for authority, returned to him as he gazed across the limpid waters to the distant islands and the remote sea whose breezes gave him life. The good fight was waged then; the battle was done. He beheld a gondola passing to some house of pleasure, and the figure of the boatman was as the figure of a friend sent by destiny to his aid. No longer would he hesitate, but cast himself from the wall and struck boldly for the ship which should be his haven.

"Signorè, for the love of God help a drowning man!"

The gondolier heard him at the first cry.

"Who is it; who is there?" he cried, ceasing to dip his oar and letting the long black boat float lazily with the current. Leopardi, notwithstanding the failing light, could see that it was a very handsome gondola. It might even belong to one of the nobles of Venice, he thought. And a noble would grant a short shrift to " The Wolf of Cismon."

"Signorè," he said, clutching the gunwale of the boat and breathing heavily, " a thousand pardons for the liberty. I am a stranger in this city and have been robbed here. They threw me from the quay yonder. For the love of God, let me find a moment's shelter on your boat."

He thought that the gondolier would answer him; but before the fellow could speak, the door of the cabin was opened, and Leopardi saw a vision surpassing any he had looked upon in all his life. It was the vision of a young girl clad from head to foot in a robe of gold brocade, — a girl whose dress was a blaze of glittering diamonds; whose mask, in her agitation, had been turned aside to show him a face so beautiful that he knew, upon the instant, he would never forget it.

"Oh, signorina," he cried, thanking Heaven for such a turn of fortune, " you will not refuse a drowning man. I am the Count of

" ' SIGNORINA, FOR THE LOVE OF GOD HELP A DROWNING MAN ! ' "

Vicenza, and I have fallen into the hands of
my enemies. Give me passage to Rialto,
and I will remember your name until my
dying day."

There was a light in the cabin of the gondola, and it stood so that the rays of the
lamp fell full upon the upturned face of
the bandit. Whether this face appealed to
the girl, or the pleasing voice of the man
attracted her, Leopardi could but surmise.
But certain it is that she stood quite still;
nor did she protest when he, quick to act
upon a resolution, dragged himself out of the
water, and sank down exhausted at her feet.

"Signorina," he said, "I kiss the hand of
my benefactress. Believe me, the hour will
come when you will not regret this night."

He touched her hand with his cold lips,
but she drew it back at once, and seated
herself again upon the cushions of the cabin.
She could see the striking face of the unknown now, with the long fair hair hanging
limp over the forehead. Wet and bedraggled
and cold as "The Wolf of Cismon" was, the
strange fascination the man could exercise
upon women was not lost to him. He held
the girl, as in the grip of his will, almost
from the first word he spoke to her.

"I will set you down at Rialto, signorè," she said quietly; "meanwhile, I fear that the cold —"

"Not so, signorina — when I am near you. A man could suffer a great deal of cold to be taken to his home under such circumstances. And I owe you yet another apology for the water I bring into your boat."

She laughed, for this strange creature, risen so strangely from the waters, had begun to amuse her.

"It will save Dominici washing the gondola to-morrow, signorè."

Leopardi sighed. He was asking himself which was the shortest way to learn the name of his benefactress.

"Do not speak of to-morrow, signorina," he said; "to-night will be a memory then. I shall have only the name —"

"The name!" she exclaimed.

"Exactly — the name of my benefactress."

She toyed with her fan, watching the bedraggled figure curiously. Her corselet shone with a blaze of precious stones. He could see the pretty white throat tuned to her rapid breathing.

"You do not know my name?" she asked.

"I am a stranger in the city, signorina."

"And you have not heard of Gabriella, of the opera?"

Leopardi suppressed an exclamation. The name of Gabriella, the singer of Milano, was known from one end of Europe to the other. He could have danced for joy when he heard it.

"Oh! signorina," he cried, "had you but sung a single note, I would never have asked you the question."

She was pleased at the compliment, for she believed that some noble uttered it. Neither the straw of the prison nor the water of the canal had ruined altogether the splendid clothes in which Leopardi had been arrested. The gold lace still flashed on his vest; the fine embroidery was still to be seen upon his coat. He would be some noble of Vicenza come to Venice for the pleasures of Carnival, she thought. It pleased her, being a woman, to think that she was helping a man who obviously had succumbed already to her beauty and her fame.

"Lord Count," she said, "I was on my way to the opera of San Samuele. Nevertheless, if I might set you down at your own lodging."

The bandit bowed with the grace of a prince.

"Signorina," he said gaily, "my way is your way. It could not be otherwise. Give me but ten minutes to call at the house of one of my friends where I can make good my misfortunes, and I will even crave leave to follow you to the opera. It is my good luck that Venice has kept this, the greatest of her pleasures, until my last night in the city."

"You quit Venice to-morrow?" she asked.

"At dawn, signorina, I shall be on my way to the mountains."

He sighed as though to say, "You could turn me from that purpose." She, on her part, had long practised all the arts which equip the successful coquette. Many a noble in Venice had laid his fortune at her feet, but this man pleased her as no other had done.

"Signorè," she said, "I will sing to-night as I have never sung before."

Leopardi answered her by entering the cabin and bending once more to kiss her hand.

"Signorina," said he, "this night will be my dying memory. We are now at Rialto.

In an hour I shall hear your voice at the opera of San Samuele."

The gondola touched the quay as he spoke. Leopardi looked about him for an instant to see if he were followed; but observing no others upon the water, he bowed again to the mistress of the boat and darted into the shadows of the narrow streets by the bridge.

"Gabriella, the singer," he said to himself, as he went. "Saint John! but my star shines to-night. Let me once get out of this cursed Venice, and she shall sing to-morrow in the camp at Cismon."

The idea pleased him. He ran on quickly down a narrow alley and into a gloomy casino.

"Quick!" he said to the man who challenged him at the door. "A message to Frà Giovanni, the Capuchin monk—and for me the best suit in your wardrobe, old Paolo. It is I, Leopardi."

The man let the lamp fall from his hand with a loud crash.

"Great God!" he said; "the dead come to life, then."

V

"The Wolf of Cismon" quitted the gloomy casino when twenty minutes had passed. Those who had seen the wet and bedraggled man as he entered, would not have recognised him when he passed out. For Leopardi wore the smirched grey coat no longer: no longer lacked a cloak for his back, nor a sword for his hand. Rich breeches and stockings of scarlet showed the fine proportions of his limbs. His doublet was of black velvet. The richest lace adorned his throat and wrists. He carried the stola of a Venetian prince over his shoulder; his vest was pinned by a diamond buckle which many a noble might have envied.

He left the casino furtively. He knew that he could not cheat Venice twice: knew that the police patrolled even that haunt of thieves and outcasts. Narrow passages, winding alleys, carried him to the water's edge. A gondola waited for him; and the boatman who steered it greeted him as a friend.

"Leopardi—as I live! Well met, comrade! I am here to take you to Mestre, as the master commands."

Leopardi leapt lightly into the boat.

" 'GREAT GOD!' HE SAID, 'THE DEAD COME TO LIFE, THEN!' "

"Well met, indeed, Beppo, my friend. You have a message for me?"

"Who sups with the wolf should breakfast with the birds. That is my message, Leopardi. The master cannot save you a second time."

Leopardi answered him earnestly.

"I will remember the name of Frà Giovanni when I have forgotten that of the mother who bore me," said he.

Old Beppo began to ply his oar, and to steer the black boat toward the Canalazzo.

"He gave you your life because you have honoured women and fed the poor, Leopardi. Remember that when you think of him in the mountains. He has been your friend, and has not forgotten his promises. You will be at Mestre before midnight, — the city thinks you dead, and the road is open."

The bandit, squatting on the gunwale at old Beppo's feet, sighed as one upon whom deep content has come.

"Oh!" he said, "I have something yet to say to this Venice of yours, old Beppo. There is Mocenigo, the judge, too. Give thanks this night that you do not wear his shoes. We go to the opera at San Samuele; there lies a better road than Mestre."

Beppo ceased to row.

"To San Samuele!" he cried. "But you are mad, Leopardi! The police are there — Mocenigo, the judge."

Leopardi encouraged him with a merry laugh.

"Barrel of Bacchus!" said he, "is it not Mocenigo who takes me to the opera? As he judged me, so will I judge him, old Beppo. And the girl I am to marry at dawn is even now waiting for me. Would you keep me from her side, rogue?"

Beppo took up his oar.

"You will hang, after all," he retorted.

VI

It had been a brilliant night at the opera of San Samuele, for this was the zenith of Carnival, and all the nobles of Venice hurried to the seats of pleasure before the stern hand of Lent should restrain them. In the foyer of the theatre the spectacle was such as even Venice, grown old in pageantry and display, had rarely known.

Princes and nobles in dazzling dresses of velvet and of silk; great dames whose very

shoes were powdered with diamonds; co-
cottes, senators, merchants, the prettiest
women in the city, — all these swelled the
glittering throng which promenaded the ves-
tibules of the theatre. The wonders of the
jewels, the superb gold and silver ornaments
of the brocades, the lights of countless diamonds, were such as blinded eyes accustomed to the wealth of Venice and to the
extravagance of her aristocrats. Strangers
stood to tell themselves that they had come
upon some palace of fables. Women hung
upon their lovers' arms, and gave themselves
up to the witchery of the hour. The babble
of tongues was deafening; the laughter
unceasing.

A bewildering scene, in truth, it was, — a
scene of folly running riot, of love grown
hysterical, of that complete abandonment to
pleasure which was characteristic of Venice
in the first years of the eighteenth century.
And this, perhaps, was even more remarkable that, in spite of the spirit of laughter
and of jest, one name was ever on the
tongue of the masqueraders. It was the
name of Leopardi of Cismon.

" He is dead," men said; "we shall remember his name no more when we cross the

mountains. 'The Wolf of Cismon' barked at Venice, and she has answered him."

So they spoke, and many paused to congratulate Mocenigo, the judge, who had helped the city to reckon so well with the bandit who had mocked her. On his part, until they told him that Leopardi was no more, Mocenigo neither slept nor ate. Impossible as the bandit's threats had seemed, they frightened this man who had willed his death. Perchance he believed the old women's tales, when they said that the rope had yet to be spun which would strangle Leopardi of the mountains. But when he knew the executioner had done his work, when he knew that the body of the robber had been cast into the lagoon, it was as though a great burden had been lifted from his mind. None laughed louder in that house of laughter. None jested with such relish.

" The Wolf is dead, my friends," he said boastingly; " to-morrow the police will have found his body, and it will hang between the columns of the Piazzetta."

Leopardi, masked closely and moving as a flash of light from place to place in the theatre, heard the words and laughed at them. Never had a reckless adventure appealed to him as this adventure did. His courage rose from minute to minute. He felt that he could look death in the face now and laugh at its menaces. He ventured even to touch the judge upon the shoulder.

" My lord," he said in a low whisper, " have you heard the news ? "

Mocenigo turned quickly.

" Signorè," he exclaimed, " the news is that Leopardi of Cismon is dead."

" Not so," answered the robber; "he has fled the prison and is now in the hills. They await you at the palace, my lord, for this man has threatened that you shall not be living at dawn to-morrow."

Mocenigo began to tremble in spite of himself. He stared at the masked man as though the sound of his voice were familiar.

" Who are you that knows the secrets of the palace ? " he asked.

" I am one who is under a great obligation to Mocenigo, the judge, my lord."

He bowed at the words, and was lost to view instantly in the press of people. The judge stared after him as though his ears had heard a voice of miracles.

"The man has fled," he muttered; "impossible. I have the word of the captain."

He would not believe it, yet doubting, and with curiosity awakened irresistibly, he passed from the theatre and came out upon the quay, whereby the gondolas waited. A boatman, who seemed to be looking for him, sprang up at once, and touched him on the arm.

"My lord," he said, "I am sent from the palace."

"You!"

"There was no other near, my lord — and the Council waits."

Mocenigo hesitated no longer. He stepped into the gondola, and it was steered instantly to the shadows. Leopardi, who watched it go, from a place upon the steps, laughed softly and returned to the theatre.

"One," he said to himself grimly; and then he thought of pretty Gabriella.

The music had begun again when he re-entered the theatre. He heard the voice of the first singer in all Italy, Gabriella of Milano, and it thrilled him as with an ecstasy of pleasures anticipated. For a little while he listened to it, and then, turning from the corridor, he entered a box,

134

where sat one of the first noblewomen in the city.

The music had swelled out now to a superb crescendo. Every ear was strained, every eye fascinated. Gabriella held the entranced audience as by a power more than human. Yet even as she rose to the supreme moment of her triumph, a terrible scream rang out in the theatre, and being repeated again and again, broke the note upon the lips of the singer, and brought the people leaping to their feet.

"Leopardi of Cismon — he is not dead. He is here, here!"

A woman uttered the words, a woman standing at the front of her box, and stretching out her arms as though for help against the apparition which terrified her. For a long minute she stood swaying there. Then she swooned and fell; and in a moment of her fall, a second cry, loud and terrible, from a box upon the opposite side, drew all eyes toward the place, and sent men's swords leaping from their scabbards.

"'The Wolf of Cismon' is in the theatre. He is here, here. There are a hundred with him. Save yourselves."

A young man, white with excitement and

passion, roared the words from the front of his box. Five hundred throats took up the cry. Women began to rush into the corridors. Flight — a flight where the strong trampled down the weak, where fathers forgot their children, a panic uncontrollable seized upon the people.

"Leopardi of Cismon is here. God help us all this night. Leopardi is here. He is not dead."

Louder and louder grew the cries. The screams of women mingled with them. Doors crashed down and barred the narrow corridors. The knife of the bandit might have been at the throat of those who fled from him. Such of the servants of the house as would have reasoned with the terror-stricken people were impotent, for panic prevailed above their appeals. Ever outward towards the crashing doors the frenzied mob poured. Jewels rained upon the carpets of the vestibule; fine clothes were rent to shreds; the weak fell swooning; the strong shouted as men possessed: "Leopardi — Leopardi is here!" Their voices were hoarse as they cried the warning.

Leopardi watched the scene from a balcony on the second floor. A curious smile played upon his handsome face. Those cries were his answer spoken to Venice which had condemned him. They were sweeter to his ears than the music little Gabriella made. And she — she had swooned upon the stage. No sooner did he realise the trouble than he climbed down from pillar to pillar; and, taking her in his strong arms, carried her swiftly through the players' door to the quay.

"Signorina," he said, when she opened her eyes, "the police are looking for you because you took Leopardi, the bandit of Cismon, into your gondola and helped him to escape."

"You — you are Leopardi, signorè?"

"I am Leopardi, signorina, who has come here to save you from the police."

She shuddered. He held her more closely in his strong embrace.

"Come," he said; "the gondola of Giovanni, the monk, is waiting for me. There will be none to stop that, signorina."

She left the city with him and was in his camp at Cismon on the dawn of the next day.

VII

THE story of the escape of Leopardi, the bandit, was believed by none of the common people of Venice, who went next morning to look for his body, hanging, as it should have been, between the columns of the Piazzetta. But when they came to the place a great cry of wonder escaped them.

" God save us ! " they said ; " there hangs Mocenigo, the judge ! "

It was a true word. The body of the judge swung there, limp and cold, in the wind of morning. And to it was pinned a paper with the words, —

" The answer of Leopardi to the city of Venice."

THE DAUGHTER OF VENICE

I

THERE were many lovers for Nina, the daughter of Barbarino, the clown, after that Venice had become her patron; but none was more persistent nor more abhorrent to her than Alvise, the jeweller. Nina said that his face was like a sheet of old copper which a smith had beaten with a hammer. She used to draw it in chalk upon the walls by which she passed when she went from her father's booth to the convent near the Arsenal. She would imitate his amatory gestures, his hoarse, croaking rhapsodies, and make the whole school laugh until there was not a dry eye in the room. And yet, in her heart, she was very much afraid of him and of her father's greed. She feared that the money-bags of old Alvise would be too much for the covetous eyes of Barbarino, the clown.

"They will make me marry him. My father will wish it," she declared to Frà Giovanni one day, when the friar came to the convent to see her. But Giovanni laughed at her.

"You are the daughter of Venice now, *Nina mia*," he said, "not even the Serene Prince could compel you to marry unless you consent. Go on with your painting and your music, and do not think of anything so foolish."

She protested with a little shrug of her pretty shoulders.

"How can I go on when they wait for me at the convent door every day, — Vittore Capello, and Leopardi, and Lando, the German count, and others? Oh, it is an army, Excellency, and I am their general. They follow me to my father's house. They bring me flowers every day, and fruit from Chioggia, and the little chains the goldsmiths make. You cannot understand these things."

Frà Giovanni shook his head. He was often at the convent of the Cistercian nuns since Venice had sent Nina there to be educated. When he did not come she wrote to him a long letter, full of her own progress, of her joys and sorrows.

"I can understand anything where little Nina is concerned," he said, amused at her strange *naïveté* and her manner of speaking;

"it would not surprise me even to hear that Alvise, the jeweller, follows her, too."

Nina became very serious.

"Oh," she said, "I do not like to tell you. Yesterday he wrote and asked me to go to Palestrina with him. He said that he would hang a rope of diamonds round my neck if I would answer him. When I left my father's house last night and crossed the bridge by the church of San Francesco, I thought that I saw him standing in the shadow. You cannot mistake Alvise, — he has the face of a wolf and his eyes are burning coals. I saw him again as I crossed our own bridge, and then I ran. It is not good to remain with the wolves when the sun has set. To-day I laugh at myself — last night I was frightened. You will not understand that, — you, who were never frightened, Excellency."

She was a pretty picture standing there in her simple dress of black cloth with white lace at her wrists and neck; but Frà Giovanni was too much occupied by his own thoughts to pay much heed to her words. Serious as the purpose of his life was, he had always loved a good jest; and the expression upon his face, as he stood there

in the hall of the convent, was one which
implied a very good jest indeed.

"Child," he exclaimed, turning to her
earnestly, "if Alvise, the jeweller, should
wait for you to-night, stop and speak to him.
Promise that you will go to Palestrina with
him to-morrow. Do not be afraid; I shall
be near you."

He spoke as though it were a matter of
very great importance; and she looked at
him for a moment with questioning eyes.
Then the truth dawned upon her, and she
burst into a merry laugh.

"Scavezzo," she cried, clapping her hands
with a child's joy, "a new Scavezzo, and he
is to be punished. I am to go to Palestrina
with him. I shall be his wife. Holy Virgin,
what a day to dream of!"

But the friar raised his finger warningly.

"Wait," he said, "we will laugh to-morrow
when you return, Nina."

II

IT was in the afternoon of the same day
that Nina paid her customary visit to her
old friends, the clowns of the Piazzetta.

When she had their news she spoke to them of many things, but always mysteriously as though she treasured a great secret.

"I cannot tell you," she exclaimed in answer to their many questions; "you will know to-night, for Frà Giovanni is passing here, and he will speak to you."

Old Barbarino, the clown, who was busy painting a mask against the day when Carnival should come again, grunted with satisfaction.

"Ha!" he said, "it is always a good day when Frà Giovanni comes to the booth of Barbarino, the clown. What lucky wind brings him here to-night, *Nina mia?*"

"No wind at all, but a wolf's head, father, which, if you scratch it properly, will shed diamonds in your hand."

Barbarino spilled a great drop of paint upon the mask, and stood with the crimson colour dripping on his own clothes.

"Body of seven lightnings!" said he, "but that is a wolf I would like to meet every day."

She laughed at his candour, and, the allotted hour passing all too swiftly, she left them at last in their perplexity. They could hear her singing, —

"*Maridite, maridite, donzela,*"

as she turned to the great square, and so towards her school in the convent of the Cistercian nuns. When she was gone, old Barbarino took up his brushes again, and began to wash the paint from the mask and from his own clothes.

"A plague on the hussy!" said he, "with her tales of wolves' heads. Who ever heard of a wolf that drove a fox from his hole? Nevertheless, my friends, the friar comes here, and we must be ready against his coming. Saint John! I could drink a flask of Chianti this night!"

He smacked his lips in pleasant anticipation and resumed his work.

Nina, meanwhile, was threading the narrow passages, and crossing the narrow bridges which would lead her to the church of San Francesco, and to the place where old Alvise, the jeweller, so often had waited for her. Still singing the people's wedding song, she ran on past the church of San Zaccaria, past the school of San Giorgio, on towards the northern quays of the city and the gardens, where the trees were green and flowers scented the air. Once she stopped to ask herself what she should say to the jeweller if he spoke to her; but she thought that the

"OLD BARBARINO, THE CLOWN, WAS BUSY PAINTING A MASK."

occasion would find the words, and so continued her journey; nor did she pause again until she crossed the bridge by the church of San Francesco and saw the jeweller himself waiting for her, as she had hoped, in the shadow of the western porch.

He was a little man with shrunken face and eagle eye. In spite of his fine clothes and the diamonds which sparkled upon his vest, he wore a hideous aspect, as of some old wolf come out of his lair at sundown. In a general way, little Nina was far too nimble to find herself embarrassed by his amatory designs; but on this occasion she lagged, as Frà Giovanni had wished, when she came to the bridge; and though her heart beat quick while she counted her strange lover's footsteps, nevertheless she permitted him to come up with her.

"Signorè," she said, stopping suddenly and confronting him, "why do you follow me? Why do you wish to speak to me?"

He bent his withered old body until the very bones seemed to crack.

"Signorina," he answered, "if you will look in the glass to-night, you will not need to ask me that question again. As for speaking to you, it is to tell you of the diamonds in the house of Alvise, the jeweller."

He put out a lean and shrunken hand and took her firmly by the wrist. No one else that she could see was in the square; and all the fears that she had imagined came surging back to frighten her.

"Signorè," she cried, feigning a child's laugh, "what have I to do with the diamonds of Alvise, the jeweller?"

He whispered his answer in her ear.

"To wear them, pretty one; to wear them — perhaps as his wife, who knows? Oh, he is rich as any in the city. And he is not too old to love you, my dear. What say you, would you see his jewels now?"

She looked round about her before she answered him. He thought that her friends were near; but she still believed herself to be alone with him.

"Not here, signorè," she said; "to-morrow at Palestrina, as you promised. I shall be in the public garden at three o'clock, — alone and waiting."

If an angel had come down from Heaven to speak of his salvation, old Alvise could not have been more surprised. A joy as the joy of youth suffused his shrivelled and hideous face. His eyes shone with a bright light. He tried to draw the girl towards him and to kiss her. But at the very moment when she began to struggle with him, a young fisherman crossed the square before the church, and stumbled so heavily against the jeweller that he reeled back into the porch as though struck by a blow.

"A plague upon your clumsy feet, rascal," he roared; "are you drunk, then, that you walk like that?"

The fisherman did not so much as glance at him. Nina herself had looked for a moment into the stranger's face and recognised him. He was Gerardo, the servant of Frà Giovanni. Someone had been near her, after all, then! She took courage at the assurance, and ran on quickly to the convent gate. But Alvise, the jeweller, watched her with the eyes of an animal.

"To-morrow," he said to himself, "to-morrow she shall see the diamonds — but they will be in my ears."

III

It was exactly half-past two o'clock on the following day when old Alvise, of the wolf's head, as the lads in Venice called him, closed his shop in the Merceria and set out to meet little Nina in the seclusion of the public garden at the eastern extremity of the city. Very early that morning he had boxed the ears of the boy who assisted him in the shop and had sent him about his business. Very early, too, he had put on his fine clothes of black satin and scarlet, and had buttoned his costly cape about his shoulders. He had worn those clothes but once before, and that was on the feast of the Ascension, when Venice wedded the Adriatic. What more fitting than that he should wear them for the second time when he, Alvise, the jeweller, would talk of marriage and of love to one whom they called the Daughter of Venice.

He had been an amorous old rogue for many a year; but, skilled as he was in those arts which win upon the love of women, he was troubled on this June day, and his hand trembled as he turned the key in the door of his shop, and set off nimbly toward the public garden. After all, Nina had powerful friends. It would never do for those friends to hear of this intrigue. Even Venice, who had become the child's patron, might be led to interfere on her behalf.

What that would mean the old man dare not contemplate. He had always been very fearful of the law and the police. He never passed the prisons without a shudder of loathing and of dread. He remembered as he threaded the narrow streets, and looked often to the right and to the left of him, that the real ruler of Venice, Frà Giovanni, went often to the convent to see the clown's daughter. The memory put a chain upon his feet; he was half of a mind to turn back again.

"Oh, come!" he said to himself, reflecting upon it, as he stood at the door of the church of San Zaccaria, "what have I to fear, after all? I will tell them I mean to marry her. And she will not have spoken to anyone. She is not such a fool. Trust the pretty jewels to blind her eyes. A clown's daughter! Odd if the law should prevent me making love to her!"

His argument revived his drooping courage. He hurried on to the public garden, and scarcely had he entered it before he saw little Nina herself, dressed so prettily in a gown of white, with a scarlet hood about her neck and shoulders, that he stood mute in admiration.

"Well," she said, — and she found it difficult to control her excitement, — "it is you, then, and the clocks struck three ten minutes ago."

He was flattered that she should reproach him for being late; and he bent his old body in a tremendous bow, while his face was lighted under its skin of parchment with the fires of his anticipations.

"Signorina," he said, "I stopped so often on my way to remind myself of your favours that I forgot the hour and the place."

He would have kissed her hand, but she snatched it from him, and ran toward the quay where a gondola was moored.

"Not here," she said, as though by-and-by he might do as he pleased with her; "wait until we are on the water. As you did not come, I called a gondola. Did I not do well, Signor Alvise?"

In spite of his haste and his pleasure, old Alvise cast a searching look at her and

at the gondola she had called. Suspicion
wrestled with him for a moment; but a man
will be blind to many obstacles when he
sets out to the pursuit of a woman, and after
an instant's hesitation he entered the boat,
and sat down beside her.

If he had not been in such a hurry, perchance the strange troubles of that day of
days would never have overtaken him. But
his haste was the haste of love, and he did
not see that the boatman, who now sent the
black gondola dancing across the lagoon,
was Gerardo, the servant of Frà Giovanni,
the same fisherman who had stumbled
against him so maliciously last night.

Unhappily for him, old Alvise was entirely
unaware of the identity of the man who
rowed him. A sense of rest and silence and
sweet content was everywhere. The jeweller pinched himself to be quite sure that he
was awake. He could not believe it even
yet; could not believe that he sat in a gondola, and that the prettiest eyes in all Venice
were looking into his own laughingly.

" Ah," he exclaimed, so soon as they were
well out on the broad of the lagoon, "so thou
hast come to old Alvise at last. I have
waited long for this day, little Nina."

His old eyes shone like reddening coals. He tried to clasp her in his arms and to kiss her; but she was quick as light, and before his hand had touched her, she stood far from him in the bow of the gondola.

"Patience, old Alvise," she cried merrily; "a little patience and I will talk to thee."

"Why do you run away from me?" he asked. "Are you not here to be kind to me to-day? Come back and hear what I have to say to you. Come back and see what old Alvise has brought for you."

She came a little way toward the awning and thrust out her hand.

"Show me the gifts you promised me," she said, tossing her little head with the air of a *bravo*.

He looked at her with astonishment in his cunning old eyes. A woman's greed was a familiar thing to him; but that this mere child should hunger for diamonds as some fine lady of Venice was like a douche upon his ardour.

"No," he said; "I will show you the jewels when you are here at my side, little Nina."

She shrugged her shoulders as though it were a matter of indifference to her.

"Oh," she said, "this is how you reward my love. What shall I say to them when I go back? How shall I tell them?"

There had been a leer of satisfaction on the old man's face until this time, but he leered no more when she had spoken. A sudden suspicion set his heart beating and brought blood to his cheeks. He turned his little red eyes upon her and she saw the light of fear in them.

"What is that? What do you say, child?" he asked sharply.

She threw herself down upon the cushion at his side, for she feared his kisses no longer. He had never seen so pretty a thing as the child who lay there resting on her elbows and looking up into his face; but his fear was greater than his passion.

"I said that I shall have a poor tale to tell to my father and to Frà Giovanni when I go home to-night."

"They knew that you were coming to Palestrina with me?"

"Certainly they did. Should I hide it from them? 'I am going to Palestrina with old Alvise, the jeweller,' I said, 'and he will give me diamonds for you.' And now — what shall I tell them, Signor Alvise?"

The jeweller clenched his hands. He could have struck her in that moment.

"Home!" he roared, climbing to his feet with the vigour of a lad, "back to Venice; do you hear me, out there?"

His words were addressed to Gerardo, the gondolier; and Gerardo answered at once.

"Certainly, signorè — but what of the others?"

"How, the others?"

"As I say, Excellency, the black gondola. It has been following us for the last ten minutes."

Had the fellow pronounced a sentence of death, the old jeweller could not have turned paler. Half believing, unwilling to believe, he drew back the curtains of the awning and looked out over the sunlit lagoon.

"The good God help me!" he cried, letting the curtain fall again; "there are the police, as he says."

Nina buried her face in a cushion that he might not see her laughing. When she looked up at him she was very serious, and the great black eyes seemed to pity him.

"Dear friend," she said, "how sorry I am

for you. It must be Frà Giovanni who has told them. They will carry you to the dungeons, and I shall never see you again."

He did not hear her. He was mumbling to himself as one whose wits had gone at the news. The police — the terrible police of Venice — were on his heels at last. He said that he might never see the sunshine again. Wild dreams of escape racked him. He drew back the curtain, went forward, and spoke to Gerardo once more.

"A hundred ducats if you get to Fusina before them," he cried. "I have friends there; they will save me."

Gerardo, the gondolier, let the lapping water play upon his oar. He did not appear to be in any hurry at all.

"It would be possible, Excellency," he said slowly; "yet how do I know that you will pay me?"

"Devil," cried the miser, "hold that purse; there are two hundred and fifty ducats in it. They are yours if I escape."

Gerardo held his oar between his knees and began deliberately to untie the leathern purse which the jeweller thrust into his hand.

"You are a generous man, Excellency, and God forbid that I should not deal honestly with you. Let us count the money now, that the signorina may be witness."

Alvise raised his hands to Heaven. The delay found the boat of the police drawing very near to them. The jeweller seemed already to feel the manacles on his wrist. He was no longer conscious that the prettiest girl in Venice sat at his side.

"Row, row!" he cried. "In pity's name, row!"

Gerardo tied up the purse with great deliberation. He took a few powerful strokes, and then stopped suddenly again.

"Excellency," he exclaimed, "in the matter of this bargain, of its conditions, and its circumstances — "

"Oh, for pity's sake — will you not row, fellow? To Fusina — I have friends there. Another hundred ducats."

Gerardo nodded his head. The long black gondola, with the police for its masters, was within a stone's throw now. The miser, gibbering, and white with terror, watched it as he would have watched an apparition of the night.

"Oh," he said, "I am lost, lost! A curse on the day. Will you not row, fellow? Do you not see them?"

" ' ROW, ROW!' HE CRIED. 'IN PITY'S NAME, ROW!'"

"If your Excellency will be pleased to point the direction —"

It was not to be borne. The driven man, snarling with anger and fear, raised his clenched fist to strike the gondolier. But before the blow fell, the other boat came up, and the Captain of the Police was at the jeweller's side.

"Alvise Falier," said he, "I arrest you in the name of the Serene Prince."

IV

THE black gondola, driven by six oars, returned to Venice swiftly. Unlike other gondolas upon the lagoon in the month of June, it had a felze, or roof for its cabin; and this cabin shielded the prisoner from the prying eyes of the curious. He sat there, dumb and paralysed with terror. The presentiment which had haunted him all his life had come true at last. He, Alvise, the jeweller, had fallen into the clutches of the police.

There were six of them in his cabin, great fellows, clothed from head to foot in black, and wearing black masks. They did not speak to the prisoner or to each other. They

sat as figures carved from ebony. Their
silence was more dreadful than their words,
old Alvise thought. He could not bring
himself to believe that he had committed any
great crime against Venice; yet this display
of the justice of Venice, these forbidding
figures, black and voiceless, chilled his very
heart.

"Signori," he pleaded at last, "where are
you taking me to; what have I done to
merit the displeasure of the Serene Prince?"

The six men bowed towards him as one,
but did not answer him, and he shrank back
from their silence with his fears made new.
When the boat had gone a little way further,
the Captain, who had arrested him, rose suddenly and clapped a bandage upon his eyes.

"A thousand excuses, signorè," he said as
he did so, "but it is in kindness to you that
I act."

It was a simple thing to do, yet if the Captain had pricked old Alvise with a sword, he
could not have been more fearful. Often
had he heard of the unnameable sights in
the dungeons of the palace. They were
taking him to those dungeons at last; and
they had put a bandage over his eyes in
mercy.

"Oh!" he said, "God help me! You are taking me to the prisons, signori?"

The Captain answered him very courteously, —

"Not so, Signor Alvise; we are taking you to the house prepared for him who is to be the husband of the Daughter of Venice."

A new light, the light of a tremendous hope, burst upon old Alvise.

"How!" he said, "Venice wishes me to marry her, then. Oh, glory be to God for that saying, signorè! Surely she shall never find a better husband."

He sat up as one made strong at the words. He could not see the smiles behind the masks of those who watched him. Nor could he learn anything from the Captain's voice when he was answered.

"Signorè," said the Captain, "it is the wish of Venice that you marry Nina, the daughter of Barbarino, the clown, after proof has been made of your goodness and of your courage. We are now at the palace where that proof shall be put to the test."

Alvise laughed like a boy.

"What an idea!" he said. "A proof of my goodness, indeed. I will soon tell them all about that, and as for my courage — "

He did not finish the sentence, for a hand was laid upon his shoulder just then, and he knew that they were leading him from the gondola and up a flight of stone steps into some building. It would be into the hall of the palace, he thought. There were no words to depict his surprise when, on the bandage being snatched from his eyes, he found himself thrust forward into a little room which was the most curious room he had ever seen.

Twelve feet square, perhaps, by as many in altitude, the room was hung from floor to ceiling in black velvet. Save for the rays of a dim lantern swinging from the black drapery of the ceiling, and for a glow of coal in a furnace, there was not a gleam of light in the place. Indeed, so dark was it that the jeweller rubbed his eyes for many moments before they showed him anything at all in the room.

When vision returned to him, he saw that the furniture of the apartment was as odd as its drapery. A brazier with live coals glowing; a pair of ominous pincers, a branding iron, a long flat wooden bench, an iron bowl, — these were the ornaments of that chamber of mysteries. Old Alvise looked at them for a moment, and then a terror past understanding seized upon him.

"The God of my fathers help me," he said; "I am in the torture-chamber, and they will burn me with that iron."

There was no greater coward in Venice than this copper-faced old rogue; no, nor any woman more timid. When he was quite sure of the things he saw, he uttered a scream which was heard half across the Piazzetta. At the same moment, one of the velvet curtains behind him was opened quickly and four men passed into the chamber.

"Signorè," the first of them said suavely, "we thought that we heard you call."

"Oh," he cried, grovelling before them, "take me from this place, signori; take me quickly."

"Not so," cried the other; "we are here to minister to your pleasures, Signor Alvise, and to further your happiness. As the doctors of Venice, we shall now put you to the proof, and see if the city may safely intrust her daughter to you."

The jeweller looked at him with eyes of terror.

"Oh," he said, "you are a doctor, then!"

"As you say, Excellency, a doctor of Bologna, and these gentlemen are my colleagues."

He pointed to the other three, who were dressed as he was. The hesitating jeweller had never seen such strange robes in all his life. Long gowns of scarlet, with odd figures painted upon them, covered the men's bodies. Sugar-loaf hats of prodigious size bobbed together as the surgeons consulted in low and menacing tones. They were all masked, and they carried strange instruments in their hands. It was impossible to take courage in such a place, and with such men. But old Alvise made a pretence of doing so.

"Well," he said, "if it is your wish to speak to me, Excellencies, I am ready."

"Not to speak to you, signorè," said the first of the surgeons, "but to make an examination of your heart, which, if you please, we would now look at."

The jeweller tried to laugh merrily.

"Oh," he said, "this is how the Serene Prince jests with me, then. Who ever heard of a man wearing his heart where a doctor could see it?"

"You will understand that presently, signorè. Meanwhile, it is our duty to proceed. Take courage; we shall deal with you as gently as possible."

He put out his hand, and grasped his prisoner by the shoulder. His three colleagues pressed round the shivering wretch, and threw him roughly on the bench, where they bound him hand and foot, and cast a cloth over his eyes. He had half believed, until this moment, that they were jesting with him as they said; but he remembered, while they bound him, how terrible the jests of Venice could be; and he cried out again with terror when the cloth covered his eyes.

"Oh," he wailed, "what are you going to do to me; what have I done that you should punish me?"

The surgeon answered him as one who comforts a child.

"Excellency," he said, "fear nothing. We are the doctors of Venice, and we understand our business. We are now about to operate upon you so that we may see your heart. But we shall pour unguents into your wounds when we have done, and you will feel nothing."

He lifted the cloth a little, that the quivering wretch might see what was going on. Alvise opened his eyes, which shone as a

madman's, and began to stare about him
wildly. He knew then that Venice had sen-
tenced him to death, and was contriving his
death in this horrid spirit of the jest she
loved so well. All round him the terrible
red hats were bobbing. He saw one of the
doctors carry in a great instrument of wood,
with a twisted handle and a sharp point of
steel; another brought the iron bowl and
put it near the torture-bench; a third stirred
the coals; a fourth sharpened a knife omi-
nously.

"Saints and angels!" he moaned, "it is
true, then; they will cut out my heart and
cast it into the water. They have done it to
many a prisoner. The Mother of God have
mercy on me! That instrument is an auger
to pierce my flesh. That bowl is for my blood.
Was ever such a punishment heard of?"

He lay very still; his lips were blue and
trembling. All that went on fascinated him
horribly. When the great instrument with
the steel point was raised above his breast,
and they tore his shirt from his bosom, he
howled as a wolf that is wounded.

"I cannot bear it!" he cried; "I cannot
bear it! Kill me and make an end, signori.
You are devils to torture a man like this."

One of the doctors, he who carried the bowl, raised his hand deprecatingly.

" Hush, hush ! " he exclaimed, " what folly is this? Are we not here to tell Venice of your courage? Take heart, then, and think upon the day of your marriage. You will suffer a little pain now; but to-morrow we shall sew up your wounds and all will be well. Play the man, Signor Alvise, I beg of you."

The prisoner's head sank back upon the wooden bench. He tried to speak to them, but no words came from his lips. When the great auger was raised above his body, he uttered a low moan, which became a resounding shriek as he felt the shining steel cut his flesh. A moment later, another pain, sharp and unmistakable, in the very centre of his back, told him that the blade had cut through his body. He listened during an instant of agony and heard a " drip, drip " into the bowl. He thought that his life's blood was flowing thus; and with one long-drawn howl of agony, he fainted.

V

It was growing dark in Venice without
when Alvise, the jeweller, came back to consciousness. The sun had disappeared behind the Western hills, and twilight hovered
for a few short minutes upon the city of
waters. But the wretched prisoner was mind-
ful neither of the hour nor of the place.
He opened his eyes in a gloomy cell, yet
could not remember how he had come to
that cell. He stared at the bed of straw
upon which he lay, at the monstrous bolts
and bars of the tremendous door, yet could
not gather any thread of circumstance which
would help his wandering mind. That he
was in one of the dungeons of the palace he
knew well. Yet how had he come there —
how?

When memory came back to him it was
swift and torturing and sudden. He did not
think of little Nina, or of his meeting in the
garden with her, or of that merry hour upon
the lagoon. The lesser facts of the day had
vanished from his mind. Only the memory
of the doctors of Bologna remained; the
terrible four who had been sent by Venice to
punish him.

" THAT HE WAS IN ONE OF THE DUNGEONS OF THE PALACE,
HE KNEW WELL."

THE DAUGHTER OF VENICE

With quivering hands he tore open his shirt and saw that his breast was red and slightly scarred. They had let him live after all, then, — these devils of the torture-chamber, — they had sewn up his wounds as they promised. Yet to what end, he asked? Was it that they might visit him with new tortures, with refinements of cruelty his mind dare not contemplate?

An hour, perhaps, passed in the contemplation of his hopeless circumstances. It was quite dark by this time and he was very hungry, — so hungry that he forgot those other fears of torture, and cried loudly that his gaolers should come to him. To his surprise, a man carrying a lantern appeared immediately in the cell. Alvise could not imagine whence or how he came, for the door did not open nor did he hear a footstep. Yet there the man stood, and his greeting was that of a servant.

"Excellency," he said, "you were pleased to call me."

"Signorè," exclaimed the trembling prisoner, "is it the wish of your master that I die of hunger?"

"Of hunger, Excellency. What an idea!

Name but the dish you would fancy, and I will bring it on the instant."

Alvise stared at the fellow in astonishment.

"Oh," he said, "I will remember your name, signorè, if ever I see my home again. Bring me a dish of fowl, and you shall find no more grateful man in Venice."

The gaoler bowed very politely.

"The price of a dish of fowl is a hundred golden ducats, signor. Give me your bond now, and I will bring it before the clock strikes again."

He spoke with assumed carelessness, as though the price named were a trifle which no rich man would think twice about. The jeweller, on his part, sat down upon his bed again and buried his face in his hands.

"It is of hunger that I am to die, then, after all," he groaned. "A hundred ducats? I have not so much money in all the world."

The gaoler laughed.

"Excellency," he said, "you think so now, but when you have been in this place for twenty hours, you will be surprised to find how rich you are. Do not make any mistake. Everything here has its price. For a dish of meat — a hundred ducats; for a pitcher of water — two hundred ducats; for wine

and candles and a bed from your own house
— five hundred ducats.   For liberty —"

Old Alvise looked up quickly.

" For liberty ! " he exclaimed.

" As I say, Excellency, for liberty, a thousand ducats."

The jeweller stood up.   He stretched out
a trembling hand for the paper which the
other held.

" Give me your bond that I may sign it,"
he said.   " I will pay the thousand ducats in
my own house this night.   God be thanked
that I should hear your words."

The gaoler slapped him on the back
cheerily.

" Ha ! " he cried.   " I knew that we had a
man of sense to deal with.   Let me hold the
lantern, signorè, while you set your name to
the paper.   I have an inkhorn at my wrist,
and here is a passable feather."

He held up the lantern, and the old man
wrote, with shaking hand, the promise that
he would pay a thousand golden ducats to
the holder of the document.

" Now," he cried, when he had signed it,
" I will go with you, signorè."

The gaoler laughed and blew out his
lantern.

"Excellency," he answered, "there is no need to go with me. Your liberty lies beyond these walls. Walk through them and you will find it."

He disappeared silently, mysteriously, as he had come. The frenzied cry of rage and anger which the old man uttered, remained unanswered. Alvise stood alone in the cell. He thought that he could hear voices beyond the walls; even the voices of women. But he knew now that Venice would never let him go. She would cheat him of his fortune and then she would kill him.

"Your liberty lies beyond these walls. Walk through them and you will find it."

Desperately he recalled the gaoler's words, and cursed the lips which had uttered them. An army, he said, could not shake the bolts of that tremendous door. And Venice had lied to him by the mouth of this jester. A miser at heart, the thought of the bond he had signed drove him to desperation. He began to pace the cell as a caged beast; he cried aloud that the man should return to him; he raised his fist and went to beat upon the great wall of stone; but at the first blow he stood thunderstruck and trembling; nor did he move a hand again until many minutes had passed.

He had struck a blow at the wall, indeed, yet his hand had fallen upon space. No stone had scarred his flesh; no jagged edges of the mortar had hurt his fingers when the blow fell. Nevertheless, there was the wall before him; there, the great door. Moonlight, rippling in the cell, showed him everything as no lantern could have done. Dazed and perplexed beyond imagination, he began to think that he was the victim of some supernatural visitation; and he shrank back to the bed affrighted and with a prayer upon his lips. Were the walls but phantoms, then? Could his gaolers move them at their pleasure? He cringed with terror at the possibility; the clock struck the new hour before he moved again.

It was nearly midnight when he recalled his gaoler's mysterious words for the second time. "Liberty beyond the walls." He repeated the promise to himself again, and began to reflect upon it a little sanely. What did the fellow mean when he said that the prisoner must walk through the great girdle of stone they had put about him? Was it altogether a jest; could there be even a grain of truth in it? Fearful still, expecting he knew not what, he rose at last from his bed and walked for the last time to the great door. A moment later he had fallen headlong through it, and lay upon the ground stupefied with fear and amazement.

"Viva, old Alvise! Viva, the lover of Nina! They have bored a hole in him, my friends, to let in some sense. What courage! What a man!"

Alvise heard the cries, but knew nothing of their meaning. Timidly he looked up and saw that he was at the very door of the booth wherein lived Barbarino, the clown, and his merry satellites. A miracle, he said; yet no miracle to the people, gathered upon the Piazzetta to welcome him. For the people knew that the cell of Alvise, the jeweller, had been made of painted cloth. They had waited patiently for him to fling himself against the mock door of it, and so to fall in the street. And now they were rewarded, in a measure heaped up and overflowing.

"Viva, old Alvise! Viva, the lover of Nina!"

All were there upon the Piazzetta,—clowns and mock doctors, and harlequins and dancing girls. Even the great instrument of torture was held aloft and lighted by the torches the masqueraders carried. The bowl, the terrible bowl, — they thrust it under the miser's nose, and he regarded it shudderingly.

It contained the red wine of Burgundy.

"Viva, Alvise! Viva, the husband of Nina!"

So the people greeted him. But the old man crept off to his home; and many a month passed before he lifted his head again, or looked upon the face of a woman.

And little Nina laughed that night as Frà Giovanni had promised her.

"Oh," she said, "they pricked his chest and pricked his back, and he believed that they had bored a hole in him."

GOLDEN ASHES

I

THE heavy key fell from the hand of the alchemist; he staggered against the door of the bookcase he had opened, and it shut behind him with a crash of glass and a splintering of wood.

"Who is there, who calls me?" he asked, as he held the taper high above his head and sought to peer into the shadows of the room. He was sure that someone had whispered his name; yet when he ventured the question, the wind answered him, — the wind and a harmony of voices floating up from the Grand Canal below his balcony.

It was a long room, the great salon of the Palazzo Balbi which Venice had given to this man, Zuane de Franza, that he, in return, might practise his arts therein and make her rich beyond the nations. A single lamp, shaded and placed upon an exquisite cabinet near the long windows, illumined the apartment at the moment when the alchemist heard a whisper of his name. He had believed himself to be alone in the room when he left his writing-table; it was nearly midnight and his servants were sleeping. Who, then, he asked himself, could have come to his house? Nevertheless, he was sure that someone had called to him from the darkness.

"Who is it, who asks for me?" he repeated, recovering himself a little, and advancing to the centre of the room.

Again there was no voice to satisfy him; only the bells of the city striking midnight in a glorious chord of silver notes, as though celestial singers heralded the morning from a hundred moonlit steeples. The alchemist counted the notes, and his heart quailed while he numbered them. Another day had begun, then! How many yet were to dawn and to die before Venice discovered the impostor she had harboured? He dare not ask himself that question.

"Pah!" he said, when the echoes floated away and his limbs were released from the trance which had fallen upon them, "the night is making a fool of me. There was no voice. I dreamed it as I have dreamed many a sight and sound since fortune sent

me to Venice. Who could be in this house
when midnight strikes? Who is there with
the courage to set foot in the laboratory of
Zuane de Franza? Fools all — there is not
one among them — ”

He turned again, with a gesture of contempt, to the bookcase for the volume he
needed. The taper showed a coarse, white
face, with a great height of forehead, and
lips thick and sensual as those of an African.
In stature short, yet with limbs that would
have been no disgrace to a workman at the
Arsenal, Zuane de Franza, clothed in his
long black gown, with fur at the wrists and
throat, was a man who would have been
marked in whatever assembly he had been
found. And there was no more persuasive
tongue in all Venice. “ I am sent from God
to bring you the gift of gold,” he had said
to the people; and the people, and with the
people, the Senate, had believed him.

He took the book from the shelf and
returned to his writing-table. When he had
blown out his taper and drawn the lamp
closer to his paper, a smile of sensuous content in his employment took possession of
him, and he forgot the voice and his own
foreboding.

"Another month, and it shall be the end," he muttered; "one more throw with the dice of life, and it shall be the last. As I came, so will I go. The fools that wait for me shall be left with their folly. The gold they seek shall be the saddle for my horse. My Elixir of Life shall stink in the flasks of Murano or wash the dead they carry to the coffins. Another month — a hundred thousand ducats yet from their Treasury — and the game is ended. The star of Franza will set, but it will rise again in another city, before another people, who will worship it as this people has done."

The thought was stimulating as wine upon the palate. He dipped his pen into the great gold inkstand before him and began to write quickly. When he had written ten lines, a memory of the voice he had forgotten came rushing back, and with it all his dread of the night, magnified tenfold, for a shadow fell suddenly across the paper still glistening with the unblotted ink. And it was the shadow of a man's hand!

Franza seemed to feel the grip of the hand upon his very heart.

"Great God!" he cried, "who is it? Who is there? Whom do you seek?"

There was no answer. The shadow vanished as it had come, swiftly, inexplicably. Yet the presence of another in the room was no longer to be doubted. The alchemist could hear a sound of breathing, even a footstep in the darkness near him. An assassin was his guest, he thought; a robber had come to his house, carried there by the wild stories that Venice told of the man who had promised her gold. No other theory was possible. And it was a theory which made good his broken courage. The terror of the unseen could bring sweat to his forehead; but of anything living he had no fear.

"Ah," he said, when he had waited a moment, and the unknown had not declared himself, "it is like that, then. You think that old Franza wears petticoats, and will pull out his purse to the first rascal who shows him the blade of a dagger. Not so, my friend, as I am going to teach you."

He stooped quickly at the words, and took a pistol, ready primed, from the drawer in the bureau at which he had been writing. The idea that he must fight for his life, with somo *bravo* sent to his house to rob him, did not trouble him at all. He would shoot the fellow as he would shoot a wolf, he said.

"You are saying your prayers, rogue?" he exclaimed, stepping suddenly toward the place where he had heard the sound of breathing. "I conjure you to be quick, or, certainly, you shall say them in purgatory. What! you would rob old Franza, the friend of Venice! A thousand devils take your impudence."

He was bold enough by this time, for his had been a life of adventure; and many a narrow plank had bridged the gulf of death for him. As he stood there in a bright circle of light, turning to this side or to that in his quest of the robber, he might himself have been some reckless cavalier of the road driven suddenly to scheme for his very liberty.

"Come out," he cried again and again; "come out and show yourself, rascal! You would rob old Franza, the alchemist! He is here, and waiting for you."

Until this moment, the unknown, whoever he was, kept to the shadows of the room. Franza could hear him moving lightly from place to place; once he thought that he saw a masked figure standing almost at his elbow. But before he could solve the amazing mystery of the presence, the point of a sword was thrust from the shadows; and so clever was the hand which held the sword that the blade struck the lock of the pistol, and fired the powder in the pan.

The report which followed seemed to shake the old house to its very foundations. The lamp upon the table, struck by the slugs, was broken into twenty pieces. A great vase fell with a crash almost at the feet of the alchemist; thick, sulphurous smoke filled the room; utter darkness prevailed, and out of the darkness a strange voice spoke.

"Signor Franza," the voice said, "what sort of a host is that who takes a pistol to welcome his best friends?"

The alchemist stood spellbound. The smoking pistol had tumbled from his hand to the floor. He could perceive a pair of bright eyes shining beneath a mask; he could see the glitter of precious stones upon the vest of the unknown; he thought that he recognised the voice of him who spoke.

"A friend!" he gasped. "How comes a friend to my house when the bells are striking midnight?"

"If he should be here to warn you, signorè?"

" 'COME OUT!' HE CRIED AGAIN AND AGAIN."

"To warn me; what warning, then, do I need?"

"The warning of one who is here to tell you that to-day Venice will demand a reckoning."

The alchemist laughed scornfully.

"How, a reckoning with me, signorè?"

"Certainly, with you who have promised her gold."

Franza began to grope his way toward his table. He sought to find a gong that he might summon his servants. But the unknown continued quickly, —

"You have promised her gold, signorè, and she, in return for that promise, has given you two hundred thousand ducats and this palace you live in. Beware how you provoke her! Beware the dawn, Signor Franza, for you may never see another!"

Franza answered him by striking the gong three times. The loud notes brought servants quickly to the room. But when the lamp was lighted again, they found their master alone, with an empty pistol and a broken vase at his feet. He, in his turn, made a poor excuse to them, and dismissed them curtly.

"To-day — the reckoning is to-day," he

muttered, when they had left him; "well, well, let it be so. The same tongue that conquered Padua shall win victory — ay, in Venice itself, though a hundred thousand were against me."

He went to one of the long windows, and opened it to pass to his balcony. It had been a glorious day of October, and Venice slept now while a world of glittering stars watched her slumbers. Below, on the Grand Canal, the long black boat of the Signori of the Night was keeping vigil of the city. Franza shuddered when he saw the boat, and closed the window quickly.

"It is an omen," he said.

II

FRANZA, accustomed to spend the night amidst the jars and phials of his splendid laboratory, slept heavily at six o'clock on the following morning when his valet called him, and, failing to wake him at the first attempt, persisted doggedly in his endeavours.

"Excellency, wake up, I beg of you; there is a messenger from the Prince, and he will not be refused."

The alchemist opened eyes heavy with sleep, and sat up in his bed.

"Well," he said, "and what did you say, Filippo?"

"That they have sent for you to go to the Palace, and will not listen to me, Excellency."

Franza lay down again.

"I have yet to learn that I am at their beck and call, Filippo. Let them come again in an hour."

Filippo, a stolid man who always spoke that which was in his mind, blurted out his news without further parley.

"Excellency," said he, "the messenger is not alone!"

"Not alone, Filippo?"

"As I say, Excellency. He is not alone."

"Then who comes with him?"

"The police, Excellency."

Franza turned as pale as the sheets upon his bed when he heard the words. In an instant the scenes of the forgotten night were remembered by him. He recalled the visit of the unknown, the mystery of the warning, the omen of the black boat lying motionless beneath his windows. A vague fear of some terrible ordeal, through which he must pass presently, haunted him to the exclusion of all other thoughts. "Beware the dawn!" the strange voice had said. He repeated the words as he dressed himself quickly. Was it true, then, that the day of reckoning had come at last; the day when he must be questioned and Venice must be answered? He would not believe it.

"Come," he said at last to his valet, while he endeavoured to assume a bold and careless manner, "you tell a tale for children. Why should the police be in this house, Filippo?"

Filippo answered him bluntly. The time for sham civilities was passed, he thought.

"Excellency," he said, "you know that Frà Giovanni preached yesterday in the church of the Frari?"

"And if he did—?"

"It was to warn them against you and your work."

All the colour left the alchemist's face for the second time that morning.

"Who is this monk," he cried fiercely, "that would come between me and the work I must do in Venice?"

"He is one who has now sent the Captain of the Police to your house, Excellency."

"Then let it be his affair and mine; and the sword decide between us."

He put on his long gown with sable at the neck and wrists of it, and made haste to descend to the great room below. Despite his fear and misgivings, he maintained that majestic and pompous manner which had won him the support of so many dupes; and he entered his laboratory with the air of a noble. The two men, who waited for him there, rose as he entered, and bowed ceremoniously to him. One was the Captain of the Doge's Guards; the other the Captain of the Police.

"Gentlemen," said the alchemist, very proudly, "I am told that the Serene Prince sends for me."

The Captain of the Guard bowed.

"At once, if you please, signorè," said he.

Franza waved his hand in acquiescence, and turned gaily to Pietro Falier, the Captain of the Police.

"Signor Falier," said he, "you will at least drink a cup of wine with me. There is need for haste, indeed, if a man must quit the Palazzo Balbi and know nothing of the wine of Cyprus lying in its cellars. It will not detain us a moment — "

The Captain of the Police answered him as the other had done.

"We must go at once, if you please, signorè," said he.

The two stood with soldiers' figures, stiff and square, as men at the drill; the alchemist could read no message on their immobile faces. Their civility perplexed him. An impatience to learn the worst began to gnaw at his mind.

"Well," he said, "if it is your wish, signori —"

"It is the wish of Venice, Excellency."

"Then Venice shall be obeyed. I am ready, sirs."

A plain black gondola carried him swiftly from his house to the Ducal Palace. By here and there the people cheered him, as was their wont. But the cries and plaudits grated on his ears. Why had the Doge sent the police to his house? Why were the honours, with which the Council of Three usually heralded his coming to the Palace, lacking?

There were many in the great square of St. Mark when the gondola came up. Clowns ran from their booths to cry "Viva Zuane!" women, hungry and ragged, blessed the man who had promised bread to the children; gallants jested with him; rich dames pressed forward to see the gold-maker.

He was accustomed to such homage, — the homage of fools to one who had duped them; but on this morning of October, in the year 1703, he had neither eyes nor ears for it. He must defend himself before the Three; he must plead for time; he must declare himself unprepared for the last, the great experiment which should enrich the city beyond her dreams. A man of dogged courage, his spirit returned to him at the thought of combat. His eloquence had won a fortune for him in three cities; it should not lose a fortune for him in Venice.

And so he entered the Palace with smiling face and ready step. That his coming had been eagerly looked for he had no doubt. He passed the guards at the Giant's Stair-case without challenge. Lackeys conducted him at once to the antechamber of the Council. A minute later he was ushered into the famous Sala dei Capi, and the President of the Three spoke to him.

It was a strange scene: the exquisite little room with the ceiling by Paolo Veronese; the aged councillors; the guards with drawn swords at the door; the secretary at the table; the solemnity, the dignity, the meaning of it all. Franza, accustomed to such scenes, bowed to the Three, and began at once to excuse himself.

"My lords," said he, "I have come here at your bidding, unceremonious though it be."

The President of the Council silenced him with a motion of his hand.

"Zuane de Franza," said he, "a year ago you came to Venice with the story that you had discovered the long-sought secret of the transmutation of metals. You brought with you water in jars which you called the *anima d'oro*, the spirit of the gold. You demanded money and a home for the purpose of your experiments. That money and that home Venice has found for you. In twelve months, you said, the waters in the jars would fructify. Yesterday the last of those months was ended. You will not be surprised, then, if to-day Venice demands the return for her hospitalities."

The alchemist heard him with a smile upon his face.

"My lord," he pleaded, "I cannot complain of your words; nevertheless, before you command me further, I would remind you

" ' MY LORDS,' SAID HE, ' I HAVE COME HERE AT YOUR BIDDING.' "

that if Venice is to reap the reward of my labours, she must be faithful to me, and wish that reward. Possibly it is unknown to you that yesterday, in the church of the Frari, the Capuchin monk, Giovanni, warned the people against me — "

" It is not unknown to us, Signor Franza. We have heard of the affair, and our officers have gone to speak to the priest you name. He has answered that, until your experiments are ended, he will promise to keep a vow of silence."

Franza shook his head slowly and pulled his long gown over his shoulders.

" That is well," he said, seeking time to think, "nevertheless, my lord — "

The President of the Three did not permit him to finish his sentence.

" Nevertheless," he exclaimed, "this is no time for excuses, signorè, but fit and proper for the fulfilment of your promises. In a room below you will find the jars of water which you entrusted to our keeping a year ago. Anything else you seek shall be brought to you. But you will understand that Venice asks a hundred thousand golden ducats, and that you must find them for her before the sun has set to-day."

Franza cried out in amazement, —

"A hundred thousand ducats, my lord! It is impossible."

"No more, no less, signorè. And since the time is short already for your task, I beg you to begin it without any further words."

He signalled to the guards at the door, and they placed themselves, one on either side of the trembling gold-maker. Franza knew not why, yet all the cunning of his tongue deserted him in that moment. He stared wildly at the motionless figures of the Three; he muttered strange words; he tried to shake the hands of the guards from his shoulders. Still gabbling incoherent excuses, he was led from the room through other galleries and other halls until at last they brought him to a narrow staircase.

"Mother of God!" he cried, "you are taking me to the dungeons?"

"To the dungeons, signorè, as you say. Yet you have but to pay Venice a hundred thousand golden ducats, and you are free to go to your home again."

He did not answer them. They could feel his limbs trembling as they led him across the bridge to the prisons which lay beyond the water. He knew well now that he could dupe Venice no more. This was the day, then, against which the masked man, who came so mysteriously to his house, had warned him. He cursed the folly which had kept him in the city an hour after that warning had been spoken.

Down and yet down, over steps green with slime and fungus; into passages where the very air breathed pestilence; by cells whence came the voices of men who had forgotten day and night and the wondrous world of stars; down and yet down into a filthy dungeon, lighted by a blazing flambeau, they carried him. As one in a dream, he saw the horrid cell, wherein the price must be paid.

"A hundred thousand golden ducats — oh, God help me, it is the half of my fortune."

But none heard him. When he looked up once more, when he recovered from the paralysing trance of fear, he was alone with the burning flambeau and the two great jars of water which he had presented to Venice a year ago. Since that day, they had been locked up as sacred treasure in the Mint of the city. The people said that they contained the *anima d'oro*, the spirit of the gold; but Franza knew better; he knew they had been filled with water from the well of his house. And here they were in his cell. Never had his own quackery seemed so pitiful to him. Venice, indeed, was a hard mistress. She would strip the very clothes from his body, he thought. Perchance, she would demand his life.

He feared death, in truth; but as yet there was no sign that Venice contemplated so terrible a punishment. He began to think that he might temporise with her. He would offer ten thousand — twenty thousand ducats. They would liberate him, perhaps, for such a payment, and he would fly the city. He would leave that very night; in Savoy, in France, it might be, he would find new dupes and new rewards. Thinking of these things, he took courage a little, and began to beat upon the door of his cell.

"Signori, I will give ten thousand ducats for my liberty. It is all my fortune. I swear it before Heaven."

The echo of his own voice was the response. Those tremendous walls cast back the words so that he seemed to mock himself. Without or within, there was no other sound than the drip of the water from one of the great jars, — from one of those jars which

Venice had carried, a year ago, with lighted candles and Host uplifted, to the cellars of the Mint. Franza looked at the jar, and a scornful laugh came to his lips. An instant later, the laugh changed to an exclamation of wonder and surprise.

"How!" he cried, "the jar overflows so that the water is above my ankles, and yet it remains full to the brim. Am I losing my eyes, then? God! what a thing to imagine!"

Cold to the marrow with the shock of that discovery, he snatched the flambeau from its iron stick and held it aloft to watch the water in the jar. Not a drop of it seemed to have passed out — and yet, the floor beneath him was running with water above his ankles. Again and again he stooped to touch the lapping stream in the cell, or to mark the jars by which he stood.

The truth was slow to come, but when it came it was as the sentence of the death that he must die. They would drown him in the cell! He knew not how or whence the water came; but he could feel it striking cold and dank upon his legs. Anon, he said, it would climb higher, would touch his knees, his breast, his neck, his chin. He cried aloud with the agony of the thought and dropped the flambeau. It hissed in the rising tide of water, and he stood in darkness.

"Signori, I will pay twenty thousand ducats for my liberty — I will sell my gold and silver — oh, in the name of mercy, I feel the water at my knees — I drown, signori!"

With darkness, a dread of death unspeakable seized upon him. He fell upon his hands and knees and crawled towards the door of the cell, cutting his knuckles as he beat upon the panel, growing hoarse with his terrible cries for help and mercy. He knew now what the justice of Venice was to those who would betray her. There, in that dank cell, with the water creeping inch by inch to his lips, he was to pay the uttermost penalty for the months of pleasure and success his roguery had earned for him.

"Signori — fifty thousand ducats for my life! I swear on the Cross that I have no more. Pity, for Heaven's sake! I am dying here, signori — hear me, help me!"

He was weak and faint at this time; faint from terror and from cold, half suffocated with the foul air which the water drove up towards the roof of the cell. His lungs pained him as though a hot iron seared them. His pulse was quick and weak; the blood seemed driven to his head; he stretched out his arms as though to seek pity of the terrible walls or to drive the darkness from him. The steady drip of the water was as a knell, — the tocsin of a death cruel beyond any he could have imagined.

Once he thought that the flow of it ceased; and then a delirium of joy began to possess him; but an instant later he knew that his strained ear had deceived him. Relentless, unmistakable, the tide was rising about him. He plunged his hands in it, and foul things fixed on them. He heard it lapping against the stones, and, in terror uncontrollable, he dashed himself against the unpitying walls and fell headlong. Any death but that, he prayed. Any death but that of the foul tide and the darkness. God would not permit such cruelty.

"A hundred thousand ducats! I will pay the money! Quick, signori, light — give me light! The water is choking me! Oh, for God's sake —!"

And then, for the first time, Venice listened to him.

Hardly had he spoken the words when some drain in the floor of the cell opened quickly, and the foul water ran back to the canal from which it had been pumped. The great trap of wood and iron swung upon its hinges. Guards with torches in their hands dragged him from the place to the light above. He came into the sunlight reeling as a drunken man. People said that he had the face of one who had lived a hundred years.

III

THAT night, at sunset, Zuane de Franza sat alone in the laboratory of his splendid palace upon the Grand Canal.

An hour ago the messengers of the Three had carried away from his house one hundred thousand ducats in gold. He could still hear the cheers of the people in the gondolas before his door. Their cries: " Viva Franza, who has made the gold ! " were as omens to his ears. The city without, then, believed that he had fulfilled his promise to Venice. He had given her gold, the people said, in return for the palace and the servants and the ducats she had found for him during the year he had been her guest. He cursed the fools who said the thing, and shut himself in his great room. He wished to be alone, that he might take counsel of the night.

He was very weak and ill at this time, and could scarce drag his weary legs up the great marble staircase of the palace. He shivered with cold, and the strong red wine he poured out for himself would not warm him. All his servants had deserted him directly they saw the boat of the Signori of the Night at the quay of his house. Even Filippo, who had been his companion in many a day of daring and of intrigue, had gone with the poltroons and the cowards who had fed upon his bounty. And he was glad of it. He must be alone, he repeated, — alone at a moment when he fled Venice, when he sought a new home and a new country, and new dupes for his cunning tongue to conquer.

It was very silent in that lonely house, and, as the shadows fell, strange shapes were conjured up of the twilight; strange figures seemed to stalk the empty rooms. Terror of the morning still haunted the broken man. He feared the things his eyes saw. When he looked at himself in a great mirror, when he saw that woeful face and the shrunken cheek and the long, dank hair, all the suffering he had endured in the unspeakable cell recurred to him. He drew back from the glass with a groan, and lay long upon a couch, quivering with fear and seeking to beat the phantoms from him.

Once or twice, as this paroxysm of terror returned, he thought that he heard footsteps in the house; and he would run wildly to the head of the staircase and cry out for his servant, Filippo. But his voice, cast back in moaning echoes, was his answer. He did not complain that it should be so. The night must find him wakeful. He had his work to do. He would cheat Venice yet, — Venice and the cursed priest who had stirred up the people against him.

A hundred thousand ducats had been the price of his freedom. It was the half of the fortune he had accumulated since he began to practise his arts in the city! The rest lay safe and snug in a great iron chest in his laboratory. If he could escape from Venice with that, he would still be a rich man. Other countries would be open to him. In Savoy, in France, he would find new dupes. This was his argument; but against it stood the haunting question, — was Venice paid in full? Would she permit him to flee? Might not the police-boat be at his door even then?

The question sent him hurrying to his balcony. He could make out the gondolas of many who went gaily to the pleasures of the night, but he did not see the boat of the Signori of the Night; nor could he espy his own gondola. Filippo had taken it, then! He, Franza, was a prisoner in his own house. He dare not trust the wreck of his fortune to the first hired barcarolo that should chance to pass his door.

He must hide his money, he said to himself, — must hide it from Venice and the Three.

Fired with this idea, he worked at the execution of it with the energy of ten men. He had no very clear notion of a hiding-place at first; but, presently, he determined to store his gold in the cellar of the palace, beneath one of the flags of the pavement which he had removed before that day to conceal some of those things which had helped him in his *rôle* of quack and seer.

Full of the excellence of his plan, he lighted lanterns and carried them to the dismal cellar; whose walls reeked of damp, whose level was below that of the water outside. It was heavy work to remove the great square stone which concealed his rude treasure-chamber; but fear gave him strength, and his very sinews seemed to crack with his efforts. He would cheat Venice yet, he promised himself; he would be revenged on the boasting monk who had denounced him. And so he worked on, and unseen eyes — the eyes of those who laughed at his labours — watched him as he worked.

Unseen eyes watched him, yet never once did he suspect that the spies of Venice were in the house. Driven on by a miser's greed, he took the golden ducats in sacks of canvas and carried them from the iron box in his laboratory to the dank and mildewed cellar.

Once, as he worked, a curious fit of terror seized upon him. A great picture, whose cord had been rotted by age, fell on the staircase just as he was about to descend with his last bag of gold. So startling was the crash, echoing in the lonely house, that he dropped the bag he was carrying and the golden coins went rolling down the stairs. He picked them up with quivering fingers, not unwilling to linger there. For he feared the darkness of the cellar; it was like a tomb, he thought. All his courage could not bring him to face it readily.

" Pah ! " he said, hesitating upon the brink

" THE GOLDEN COINS WENT ROLLING DOWN THE STAIRS. "

of the lower steps, "what am I thinking of? I that have been feared in my own house! Let them come if they choose; let them do what they will with me. A hundred thousand ducats will pay the bill at many an inn. They shall carry me to France, and I will promise gold to the French King. I will begin again and make good the fortune I have lost. While men's greed remains, there will always be a home for Franza, the gold-maker."

He stooped again to the bag and went down to the cellar quickly. When he had poured the last of the gold coins into the cavity, a mighty effort forced the stone back to its place, and a low cry of joy escaped him.

" To-morrow," he said, " to-morrow Filippo will return, and together — God, what is that?"

The word of triumph ended in broken exclamation. He had hung a lantern upon a hook in the wall of the cellar, and it cast a poor ray of wan light on the pavement beneath which his fortune lay. That which caused him to cry out suddenly was a shadow upon this patch of light. He saw that it was the shadow of a man, and he watched it with outstanding eyes, and remembered the warning of yesternight, which he had long forgotten. All his false strength left him in an instant. He sank upon his knees; he uttered a low moan as of ultimate woe and pain.

"What is it — what do you want with me?" he asked pitifully.

Again, as last night, a voice answered him out of the darkness, —

"A hundred thousand ducats, in the name of Venice, signorè, — the hundred thousand you have just hidden beneath that stone."

Franza groaned aloud; his hands were outstretched before him; he seemed bent to the very earth by this new blow.

"Who are you that came yesterday as a friend, but to-day are an enemy?" he asked.

"Yesterday I stood for the mercy of Venice, signorè; to-day I stand for its justice."

"Is it justice that I, who have paid a hundred thousand ducats this morning, shall pay yet again?"

"A hundred thousand a day — so you promised Venice a year ago, signorè. And a new day has come. Hark to the bells, they are striking twelve!"

Franza listened to the sweet music floating over the still lagoon. He shuddered as he heard the bells.

"I will pay the money," he said in a low voice — "take it, signorè; it is beneath this stone."

The unknown laughed softly.

"Not so," he said. "Venice is no bandit, Signor Franza. You shall yourself lift the stone and count the money into my hand."

"But I am weak, signorè; all my strength is gone. I am as a child."

"That is your misfortune, then. It is a very great misfortune indeed, signorè, for if you do not pay me that which I am sent to ask here and now, you will not be alive when the clock strikes again."

Franza breathed heavily. He staggered to his feet, and turned to the place whence the voice came.

"Who are you that comes to torment me? In God's name, speak."

A man stepped from the shadows. He was clothed from head to foot in scarlet, and wore a scarlet mask. He carried a naked sword in his hand.

"Signorè," said he, "I am the executioner of Venice."

Franza drew back from the apparition

step by step. He covered his eyes to shut it out; he tried to speak, but could not articulate his words. He knew that the end of his life had come; but to die there, in that cellar, to die with no prayer upon his lips, to know that his head would roll upon that slime-dewed floor, — it was a fear of death surpassing all imagination.

"I cannot die," he moaned; "I cannot die here — in this place."

"Not so," said the other; "you should have asked mercy of him who is the voice of Venice, signorè."

Franza cast himself upon his knees.

"I ask it," he cried, cringing in the very dirt of the pavement. "I ask it of Giovanni, the lord of Venice."

"Whom you denounced this morning, and compelled to take a vow of silence! How shall he pardon you when he may not speak of you to anyone until another day has dawned and set? It is not to be, signorè. Prepare for death, for you have not a minute of life!"

He raised his hand, and other figures emerged from the darkness. Men, dressed in red and masked as the executioner was, seized the wretched gold-maker and dragged him from the ground. A block of wood was thrown carelessly to the floor; they forced the head of their prisoner down to it; they held him by the arms in an iron grip. His terrible cries fell on ears that might not hear. He waited for the blow, waited to feel the steel cutting through his neck — yet no blow fell.

"Strike," he implored; "in the name of God, strike!"

But the sword did not fall. Those instants of delay, with the shining blade poised above him, were eternities of suffering. A thousand deaths he died, and everyone was an agony surpassing the others.

"Oh!" he cried, "strike if you are not devils. I will die — I will — "

They did not answer him; and he rolled, fainting, from their arms; for he had passed the bounds of suffering and of fear.

IV

EARLY on the next day, one of the gondolas belonging to the police of Venice left the Palazzo Balbi to set down upon the mainland an old man clothed in rags, and thankful for the morsel of bread and the cup of wine which his gaolers gave to him. When the boatmen had set him ashore, the unwilling traveller limped with pain along the deserted shore, and as he went, he looked back often toward the blue lagoon, above which the spires and domes of Venice rose gloriously in the morning light.

"She has repaid," he said, shaking his fist at the distant city, "God knows, she has repaid."

And so Zuane de Franza, the alchemist, started on his journey towards a new home and a new country.

WHITE WINGS TO THE RAVEN

I

A T eventide on the 3rd day of April, in
the year 1706, the Palace of Bianca,
Marchesa della Scala, was lighted from
garret to cellar; and word soon went round
that another of those great feasts, which had
been the envy of Italy, was about to be cele-
brated in her house. Nor was the surmise
an incorrect one. Scarcely had the sun gone
down behind Chioggia when the loiterers
upon the bridge by the church of Santa
Maria Zobenigo began to number the gondolas, and to name the guests they set down
at Bianca's door.

Such a splendour of gold and silver and
precious stones, they said, could be seen at
no other house in the city. It was a delight
to them to hear the distant music, and to
watch the pretty women, and to imagine all
the joys of eating and drinking and love-
making which the gloomy walls of the palace
hid from their eyes. For Bianca was the

Queen of Venice in her way, — a queen to whom even senators had paid homage; a queen whose wealth seemed inexhaustible; whose beauty had been the theme of poets even in the distant capitals.

It was a merry crowd upon the bridge, and the passing minutes added to its numbers.

Here was a boatman whose day's work was done; there an honest glass-blower from Murano; yonder a hussy seeking a lover; or, again, a well-dressed stranger, who kept his cloak about his face and exchanged words with none. All feasted their eyes on the splendid procession which now passed up the steps of the palace to the throne room of the woman who had conquered Venice so indisputably. Wit and scorn and merriment were mingled in the running fire of exclamation with which each new guest was greeted. It was the people's privilege to be critics, and they spared none in their liberty.

"There goes fat Moriale and his wife with him. By Bacchus! he will get his ears boxed right well to-morrow, for the compliments he is about to pay the little witch upstairs."

"Pah! as well ask a wine-cask to go down on one knee. He dates his writing from the last year he saw his feet. Look rather at old Vittore Capello, who goes up the steps with the toes of a goat. I 'll wager a *scudo* that he will kiss pretty Bianca behind the curtains before he comes down again."

"Saint John!" cried another, "his pockets will be light enough at dawn to-morrow, comrade. Name the rich man that pretty Bianca has not diced out of his money, and I will vow a *novena* at the Altar of our Lady of Miracles."

A young boatman, turning away scornfully, expressed a thought which was in the mind of many of those honest citizens.

"For my part," said he, "I would sooner hang between the columns of St. Mark than call that great lady my mother."

"Well spoken, Gentile," said a good-humoured innkeeper, who had listened with interest to their talk; "it is an ill day for Venice when she harbours such hawks as the Marchesa della Scala."

"Where is her son," asked another, "why is he silent when his mother's name is in the mouth of every wanton? I remember the day, signori, when there was no greater house in Venice than that of the Marchese della

Scala. The poor fed at his tables; the Senate listened to his words. And now — look you — it is a house of devils, and the woman you speak of is their queen."

"To God be the glory that her son does not know," was the answer of the jeweller, who had just come up. "He is in France, signori, and who shall tell him how the sheep go to the shearing in that great house? Not I — nor the priests she drives from the churches, nor the poor who die on her doorstep, nor the merry men she has sent to the dagger and the sea. Let well alone. Some day Venice will reckon with her, and then!"

A loud chord of music from the open windows of the palace cut short the satisfaction with which these opinions were received. Men pressed to the parapet of the bridge to watch other gondolas as they set down their glittering burdens on the quay of the brilliantly-lighted house. Young girls exclaimed with delight, as women, whose jewels would have set a new king upon his throne, passed up the steps to the saturnalia awaiting them beyond the threshold; beggars drew their rags closer about their bodies, while gallants, in breeches of satin, and coats of gold brocade, and vests sparkling with diamonds, stood a moment to prepare their compliments to the pretty Bianca.

In all that little crowd there were but two men who betrayed no further interest in the Palazzo della Scala or in its people. One was the stranger, who had drawn his cloak about his face when first he had come to the bridge; the other was a cowled friar, who watched the unknown youth rather than the quay to which the eyes of the boatmen were turned.

The two men quitted the bridge together, crossing it towards the *campo* before the doors of the church. They had left the echoes of the music and the laughter far behind them before the stranger knew that he was followed; but so soon as he heard the footsteps of the friar, he turned angrily and demanded his business.

"Signorè," said the friar, throwing back his capuce that the other might see his face, " my business is with the Marchese della Scala."

The unknown started and laid a hand upon the hilt of his dagger.

"The Marchese della Scala," he cried; "then seek elsewhere, brother, for I know not the name."

"In the shadow of your mother's house, you do well to forget it, my lord; but here, here where none may listen, you will remember that it was the greatest of the great names of Venice."

The youth, for such the unknown was, leant against the door of the church and buried his face in his hands.

"God help me, signorè!" he said with a deep sob; "she is my mother."

For a little while the friar did not speak. His heart was heavy for this handsome, open-faced lad whose father, years ago, had been his own good comrade of the old days at Iseo. When he spoke again, it was almost with the tenderness of a woman.

"My son," he said, "think not that any idle curiosity brings me to your side to-night. I am here but for one purpose. It is to give you back the name you have lost."

The young marquis looked up quickly.

"What miracle gives white wings to the raven, signorè? Answer me that, and I will listen to you."

"A miracle of love, signorè, — the love which sleeps, but which to-morrow will awaken."

He spoke very earnestly, laying his hand

gently on the young man's arm. There was something in the tone of his voice which filled the other with a hope and confidence such as he had not known for many years.

"Brother," he said, "who are you that you should wish to help me or to remember my name?"

The priest answered almost in a whisper.

"In this city I am known as Frà Giovanni," he said, "but your father knew me as the Prince of Iseo, signorè."

The young marquis uttered a cry of wonder.

"Frà Giovanni!" he cried; "you are Frà Giovanni! Surely God has heard my prayer, signorè. There is no city so distant that the name of the Master of Venice is not spoken there with love and reverence. If he should prove my friend!"

The priest answered by linking his arm in that of the young man and leading him toward the Piazzetta and the Ducal Palace.

"Marchese," he said, "the feast of the Ascension shall not be here before I say to you, as my Master said to the apostle he loved, 'Son, behold thy mother!'"

II

Twenty days had passed, and the name of Bianca, Marchesa della Scala, was again upon the tongue of the Venetians. For the feast of St. Mark the Evangelist drew near, and people said that the mistress of Venice would keep it as never feast was kept before. Every great noble of the city, the patriarch who ruled the Church, the president who ruled the judges, the admirals of the fleet, the generals of the armies, the lords of Vicenza, of Padua, of Brescia, of Florence, — all these fell under Bianca's spell and promised her support. It would be an orgy surpassing words, the common people said. But others shrugged their shoulders and cried: " Shame on Venice, that she should honour one who has made our rich men poor; shame on the woman who has taught our sons that the dice-box is greater than the sword."

Frà Giovanni heard of these boasts and kept his peace. The whole city was against him, he said; nevertheless, he gave vague words when people spoke of the Palazzo della Scala, and to one he said: " My son, the feast of St. Mark shall find the Marchesa della Scala beyond the mountains of Vicenza."

He uttered the threat, nevertheless, and the twentieth day was nearly done before he seemed again to remember the name of the woman or his promise to her son. On the eve of the feast of St. Mark, however, he quitted the Island of the Guidecca, where his home was; and going alone in his gondola, about an hour before the Angelus, he set out for the Palazzo della Scala and knocked boldly at its door.

The great house was all confusion then. Lackeys tumbled over lackeys; cooks bawled their commands to cooks; the antechambers were loaded with palms and fine glasses and hangings of the richest cloth; the workmen were building the galleries for the musicians; gondolas came unceasingly to the quay of the palace with some new burden which should add to the splendour of the feast. But none paid heed to the cowled monk, who stood timidly at the door of the great house.

"We have no time for such as you," said a lackey who answered him; "go back to your cell, brother, lest your eyes be tempted by the things you see."

The priest threw back his cowl.

"Not so, my friend," he said sternly; "but do you go up to your mistress and carry my message, or to-morrow might find you without a tongue to utter it."

The lackey, recognising the speaker, fell on his knees before him.

"Excellency — I did not know you; I will carry your message — if you had but shown me your face before."

The answer was a gesture of impatience.

"Tell none that I am here," said the priest, sternly; "to your mistress say that a brother of the Capuchins waits below with news from Savoy."

The lackey hastened up the stairs, glad to prove his diligence. A moment later he returned and began to make his excuses.

"Excellency," he said, "my mistress will see no one."

"Go again," said the friar, angrily; "I come from Savoy and bear a message from him who should be the master of this house."

The lackey ascended the stairs for the second time; but Frà Giovanni now followed upon his heels. In a little alcove on the first landing, an alcove where workmen were erecting a booth of flowers, the priest came face to face with Bianca herself. He stood silent for a moment, so great was the fascination of her beauty. He knew that she must be in her fortieth year, yet she had the face and figure of a girl of twenty.

"Signora," he said, bowing gravely, "I am a brother of the Capuchins, and I come to tell you that your son has need of you in Turin."

He spoke as though he wished to pay her great homage; but she turned upon him in one of those sudden bursts of anger which had humbled even the great men of Venice.

"Has my son no other messenger," she cried, "that he must send such as you to my house? Beware, lest my servants whip you from the door, signorè."

The priest did not flinch.

"Signora," he said gently, "he is your only son, and he is in trouble. It is strange that he should remember his mother's name when other names have been forgotten."

She raised her hands and clenched them.

"Oh," she cried, "a mummer in the habit of a priest. A mummer who dares me in my own house —"

"Nay, signora, say rather the messenger of God, who comes to warn you that your hour is at hand; who comes to tell you of the poor who hunger and the sick who die; who craves mercy of you for one that loves; who sees light in your house but darkness in the homes of Venice; who hears the cry of the children and would that you should hear it too. A mummer, indeed, but the play is holy, signora, and the finger of Almighty God has written it."

He drew his cowl close about his face and turned upon his heel. She watched him with a hand at her throat and anger passing words in her heart.

For it seemed, when he was gone, that someone had written upon the wall of the great house the sentence of its doom.

III

THE day of days, the feast of Mark the Evangelist, dawned angrily over Venice. A great blight seemed to fall upon the city; thunder-clouds hovered about the distant mountains of the mainland, and loomed over the waveless lagoon. Nevertheless, there was a little burst of sunshine at six o'clock in the morning; and another hour had not passed before men, and women, too, forgot the hour and the day, and thought only of the news, surpassing belief, which spread as a pestilence through all the places where the citizens loved to congregate.

An acolyte of the great Ducal Chapel, going leisurely to Mass at five o'clock in the morning, had been the first to see the thing; and so greatly had it surprised him that he ran quickly to Scavezzo, the fat canon, and blurted it out, regardless of the holy building or of the Mass which was about to begin.

"Oh, Excellency, Excellency, someone has written strange things between the columns of the Piazzetta. It is the list of the guests who were to go to-night to the house of the Marchesa della Scala."

Scavezzo was putting on his vestments when the lad spoke, but he let go the girdle of his alb at the words and crossed himself hastily.

"What!" he cried, "the names of the guests of pretty Bianca written over the place of execution! God save us all this day!"

Never had he heard such tidings. Unable to restrain his curiosity, he ran quickly across the great square, and so to the Piazzetta, where stand the two columns between which the criminals of Venice perished. A crowd had gathered already about the marble slab whereon they laid the severed heads of the condemned; and these people discussed with awe and wonder the strange event which the night had brought about. When Scavezzo appeared among them, they hailed him with delight as one who could explain the mystery.

"Here, my lord, the paper is here. They have set it on the slab where runs the blood of murderers. Look for yourself: it is a list of those who have been invited to-night to the house of the Marchesa della Scala, — a list of her guests, and sealed with the great seal of the city!"

Scavezzo stood panting, but he would not touch the paper.

"My children," he said, "be sure that the police have put that paper where it lies, and that it is not for such hands as ours to touch it. I am sorry for the Marchesa della Scala, for who will go to her house when this is known? Surely the justice of Venice is very hard that it should thus visit one who, I do not deny it, is a little fond of the dice-box, yet whose banquets are not surpassed in Italy. Be advised of me, my friends, and go to your homes. There is danger in the air to-day, and the wise man will not wish to breathe it."

He uttered a heavy sigh, for the memory of pretty Bianca's good wines was very dear to him. But the people continued to discuss a discovery so momentous long after he had returned reluctantly to the altar awaiting him.

"Venice will send a message to Bianca to-day, my friends. Our Father Giovanni has spoken at last. We shall hear of her banquets no more. And God help those who go to her house to-night!"

They hurried to their homes, speaking of the thing in whispers. Soon the news spread from house to house, was whispered in palace and in garret; was muttered in the confessional, and remembered by priests before the altar. Even the patronage of the nobles of Venice had not saved Bianca from the anger of the great friar, men said. What of her banquet now? they asked. Who would pass her doors when he had read his name written there on that pavement which the blood of the guilty had dyed?

The news spread from house to house, yet none was so bold that he whispered it in the Palazzo della Scala. Fearing they knew not what vengeance of the police, even the workmen, who came in the morning to finish the task of preparation and display, held their tongues. If the servants of the great house had learnt the tidings, they dared not whisper them to their mistress. Slowly, silently, the work of decoration went on. And in her own room Bianca, dressed as she had never dressed before, told herself that the victory was already won. " To-night," she said, " to-night Venice shall be at my feet."

Punctually at a quarter to eight o'clock she entered the great salon upon the first floor, and prepared to receive her guests. Superb as the decorations of the great apartment were, the mistress of it was worthy of her lavish surroundings. A robe of gold brocade fell from her pretty white shoulders to her feet; her girdle was a girdle of diamonds. The finest pearls from Hungary shone white upon her snow-white throat; a great diadem of flashing jewels sparkled above her auburn hair. No better-shaped hands nor arms had been seen in Venice, the painters said. Hands and arms now glittered with the wealth of the gems they carried. In her deep blue eyes those about her discerned the look of one who had triumphed. A flush was upon her cheeks, — the flush of victory assured.

She entered the great ballroom of the palace at a quarter to eight, and one searching glance satisfied her that all things were, indeed, well done. In the gallery at the northern end musicians already were seated. Banks of white and crimson flowers stood to screen the orchestra. Thousands of candles in glass chandeliers warmed the room to rich colours with their mellow light. Lackeys in liveries of scarlet and of blue waited at the head of the great marble staircase to announce the first of the guests. Bianca said that the spectacle was worthy of her house. She turned for a moment to see her own figure where a great mirror caught it up; and a content surpassing any she had known came upon her.

" I have kept my word," she thought. " Venice shall bear witness to-morrow."

A quarter of an hour passed in this task of inspection. When she had satisfied herself that all was well, the great bell of the church of Santa Maria Zobenigo began to strike the hour of eight. She counted the strokes, and a strange sense of uneasiness came to her of the notes. Eight o'clock, and no one in her house! What dilatory fit had overtaken her guests, she asked? Even the lackeys at the door had begun to fidget; and one of them went to the balcony as though to arrange a curtain, but in reality to look out upon the canal below. Very much to his astonishment, the fellow observed that there was not so much as a single gondola at the quay of the house. But a great crowd stood upon the neighbouring bridge, and he could hear the buzz of its excited talk.

"They are coming, Leonardi; the boats are below?"

"There is no one there, Excellenza."

The Marchesa asked the question of that lackey with an assumption of an indifference she was far from feeling. That premonition which is a factor of so many misfortunes warned her already that something was amiss. It was no great matter that the first of her guests should be a few minutes late — and yet —

"Do you not hear the bell?" she asked her servant presently.

"I hear nothing but the voices on the bridge, Excellenza."

A crimson flush dyed her cheeks. She opened her fan and began to use it briskly.

The lackeys on the stairs without were talking in low whispers. The bell of the church of Santa Maria struck a quarter past eight.

Bianca went to the window of her balcony and stood there breathing quickly. The crowd on the neighbouring bridge saw her, and hailed her with derisive cries. There came to her in that instant a memory of the priest and of his warning, which she had forgotten.

"Oh," she said, "what is it, what does it mean? Who is keeping them away? What story have they heard?"

She did not know at this time what she feared, or why her guests delayed their coming. Many excuses for them were suggested by her busy brain; but in spite of it all a vague foreboding crept upon her, and she still thought that she heard the voice of the priest warning her. Often she asked Leonardi if he did not hear the great bell of the house; his answer was ever the same:

"There is no one there, Excellenza; there is no boat upon the canal, only the people on the bridge."

Half-past eight o'clock was the hour now, and as it struck panic seized the mistress of the house, and was shared by her servants.

One by one they began to leave the palace: at first the more timid and impudent; then the irresolute; at last even those whom she had trusted greatly. Alone there in that great ballroom, alone with the countless tapers, and the sweet-smelling flowers, and the gold and silver of the ornaments, she stood as one in a dream. The message which the night gave to her was the message the priest had spoken. "Your hour is at hand," he had said.

For a little while the absence of her servants was unnoticed. When she discovered it, when her voice began to echo through the empty rooms, and was unanswered, when pitifully it changed from the voice of an angry woman to the cry of one in great trouble, the full significance of the night was revealed to her. She knew that the Three had willed this punishment. Some enemy had warned the people to shun her house. She began to ask what other punishments awaited her. She ran from room to room hysterically, as though some befriending voice would speak to her there. She returned again to the head of the great staircase and stood there as one petrified.

For guests were coming to her house now.

They were already upon the marble staircase. They swarmed up as an army to the loot. Their cries were as the cries of demons. They were the beggars of Venice, — ragged, haggard, hungry.

The woman stood without the power of voice or limb; it seemed to her that her very heart was paralysed. She had heard of these people, — the children of the Ghetto, the children of the factories, the bravos from the Ambassadors' kitchen, the thieves, the assassins, the honest poor of Venice, — but never had her dainty eyes been permitted to see them.

She knew that this was her punishment, this the ultimate humiliation that Venice had put upon her. Where the great lords of the city should have stood, the ragged, the homeless, the starving, now bent their knees in mockery. With joyous cries and the frenzy of plenty anticipated, they crowded about the mistress of the palace.

" Viva, Bianca! Viva, the Queen of the Poor! Viva, our Lady of Venice! The tables are spread, comrades; the wine is ready."

The very pit of the nether world seemed open in that house. Gaunt men; *lazzaroni* whose rags scarce hung upon their shoulders; cripples, whose bent limbs wormed, beastlike, upon the stairs; women with the faces of witches; outcasts whose eyes were alight with the fires of hunger; children old in deformity, and pain, — all these swarmed about the mistress of the palace. They breathed their thanks into her ashen face; their rags were pressed to her robe of gold; their shouts resounded in the house. They kissed her hand: they knelt to her; they swept by as a torrent to the place where the flagons were filled and the feast was ready.

But Bianca fell in a swoon, and the beggars passed triumphantly to the tables awaiting them.

IV

THE last of the guests whom Venice had sent to the Palazzo della Scala left the house when the neighbouring clocks were striking the hour of midnight. Bianca heard their shouts as they swarmed away in boats and barges; she heard the greetings they passed with those on the bridge. In the solitude of that great ballroom she looked at the trampled flowers, at the tapers guttering in their sockets, at the crumbs of the feast which was to have been the glory of Venice. But she neither wept nor spoke. A vague sense of personal peril, a shrinking from the fatal truth which must be known to-morrow, were her prevailing thoughts. She moved as some spirit of the feast, as some apparition, going from room to room and door to door, saying always, " I am alone."

Venice had humiliated her; she knew that no further humiliation was possible. Never again would she hold up her head in the city; never again would her name be aught but sport for the people, — a mockery and a name dishonoured. Woman-like, she cared less for any punishment that her judges might be about to visit upon her than for this mortal wound to her vanity. And, woman-like, too, she began to long in her heart for some word of sympathy, if it were but one which should loose the imprisoned tears and open the salving torrent of her grief.

" Oh, my God," she exclaimed, " help me, for I am helpless and alone ! "

A voice answered her, speaking from the shadows. She recognised it at once and stood up quickly when she heard it. The pride of Bianca of Venice was not yet broken.

"Signora," said the voice, "it is God's will that I come here to answer your prayer."

The speaker stepped to the light, and she beheld the cowled friar who had come to her upon the eve of the feast. But his voice was no longer the voice of one who judged her; he spoke with gentleness as a brother who pities and would comfort.

"Who are you; why do you come here?" she asked, struggling the while with her pride, yet turning toward this unknown as to one sent from the darkness of the city to be her friend.

Frà Giovanni, for he it was who now stood before her, threw back his robe that she might see his face.

"Signora," he said, "I am one whom they call the father of Venice; and I come to help you even as I helped your husband long years ago at Brescia."

She looked at him with wonder in her eyes.

"I know you," she said in a low voice; "you are the Prince of Iseo."

The priest covered his face again.

" The Prince of Iseo, as you say, signora
— yet, to this city, the Capuchin monk,
Giovanni, who comes here to-night to help
you, as last night he came to warn you."

" To help me, my lord; you come to
help me. Nay, look upon this house and
tell me what help can save my name now."

" Signora," he said earnestly, " we go
where you shall build you a new house and
a new name. Come quickly, for my gondola
waits at the *riva*."

They quitted the Palazzo della Scala together before ten minutes had passed. She
knew not why she went nor whither; but it
seemed to her that this priest, who had been
her husband's friend, would befriend her in
that hour of her necessity. Ever in her
mind was the thought of her humiliation and
of the new day to come. What vengeance
did the city yet contemplate? It might
even contemplate her death, she thought;
and to such a one the fear of death was a
dread unspeakable.

Whither, then, did the priest carry her?
She asked the question silently as the gondola turned from the great Canalazzo to one
of the narrowest and the most pestilent of
the water-ways of Venice. Fearfully she

looked up to the great silent houses, to the alleys, and the stinking dens of the poor which bordered them. There were moments when she distrusted the man, and feared even that he was conducting her to the prisons.

Through the narrow water-ways, by the church of La Madalena, on past San Marcuola, toward the Ghetto and the ultimate west. How should she find help in such a place of misery and of want, of hunger and of crime? For she was in the beggars' city now. Here lived the very poorest in Venice. She had heard of the place as of some pit of horrors; but now her eyes must look upon it to read its truths for themselves. When the gondola stopped at last, it was before a wretched house, into whose lower rooms she could see quite plainly. A young woman lived there, and the wan light of a candle showed her white face bending over the cot where slept her child.

" Look," said the priest in a low voice, "an hour ago that woman was your guest, signora. But she neither ate nor drank. Her thoughts were in that room with her son who slept. See now what gladness has come into her home. For she has carried your gifts to her child — and the child will live."

Bianca buried her face in her hands. Swiftly there came to her the memory that she, too, had a son, and that he had waited vainly to hear her voice.

"Signorè, for pity's sake spare me!" she exclaimed; "my son waits for me in Turin."

Again the gondola shot over the dark waters of the fetid canal. Again it stood before the windows of a house. A lamp swung from a ceiling blackened by age and smoke. A bed of rags stood near a stove; an old woman, whose white hairs were as an ornament of silver to the room, lay in the bed. Squatting on the floor was a cripple, whose twisted and distorted limbs had climbed the staircase of the Palazzo della Scala but an hour ago.

"Look," said the priest, as he touched the arm of the trembling woman, "a son whom God has cursed, for so the people say, carries bread and wine from your table to the mother who bore him. What happiness is in his heart to-night because of the feast you gave, signora! Call it not a humiliation, then, to have done as Christ our Master did before us. Can there be humiliation because the children live and the hungry are hungry no more? Nay, say rather that it is a work of God, most blessed, to which you have been sent."

The gondola passed on swiftly. Bianca sat white and still, for a new world and the visions of a new world were unfolding before her eyes. She saw the cities of the poor, the cities of the little children; she saw the throne of her motherhood, and the name of her own son was upon her lips. She did not hear the priest when he bade her look for the third time.

They had stopped before a small house near the church of San Geremia. The door of the house was open. In the stone corridor beyond, a little coffin, with tapers on either side of it, awaited the boat which should carry it to San Michele.

"Signora," said the priest, dropping his voice until it was but a whisper, "look well, for yonder is a house of weeping. He was their only son, and the least of the jewels you wear would have given him back to them. Never more in that house will a child's voice be heard nor the word of a mother to him she loved. Oh, look upon it well, signora, for the tears fall upon the child's face as to-morrow they may fall upon the face of your son."

He spoke as one who judges, for he knew that the hour of his victory was at hand. When he had finished, he looked at the woman and saw that the burning tears were falling fast upon her hands. Pride warred with her grief no more. All the years she had reigned in Venice were forgotten in that instant. She was a woman crying for the love of the child she had lost.

" God," she prayed, " if I might live to see my son again."

The priest heard the prayer, and pity welled up in his heart.

" Signora," he said, " how many women in Venice have that prayer on their lips to-night — and shall be unanswered ? "

She cringed at his words, and a cry, as of a woman who has known all that human suffering can teach, escaped her lips. The jewels at her throat seemed to burn her. " They would give life to the children of Venice," she thought.

" Take me to my son," she cried. " To-morrow I will find a home in the convent of Murano. The children of Venice shall hunger no more —"

"Signora," was the answer, "your home lies in the houses of the poor."

He made a sign to his servant, and the gondola was halted at the steps by the bridge of Rialto. A young man stepped from the shadows of the quay when the boat came up; he raised the weeping woman and held her in his strong arms.

And to him the priest said, as he had promised to say, —

"Son, behold thy mother!"

THE HAUNTED GONDOLA

I

THERE had been a growing fear of the mystery for many days, but when the Feast of the Ascension came at last, panic fell upon the city; and even the voices of the priests were powerless to control the terror of the people. Strangers coming to Venice stood awestruck in the great square, unable to believe that this was the city of their dreams. No bells rang out a joyous welcome to the weary traveller; no processions passed from the splendid churches; no clowns fooled upon the Piazzetta; no music was heard upon the lonely waters. Even the palaces of the rich were closed, and by the alleys where the poor herded, prophets stood to cry, "Woe to Venice, for the Day of Judgment is at hand!"

There had been a growing fear of the mystery; yet none could say why he feared or what enemy had come down to the city to strike at the best of her sons and the wisest of her councillors. Nevertheless, men said that death was everywhere, — death by the poniard, death of a strange sickness, the swift lurking death which struck unseen and paid no penalties.

At first mere gossip to make chatter for the day, the story of another victim killed by a bravo, the dread of the sickness of the East, men found it no more than the common peril of the age they lived in. But anon it took a swift and terrible turn, — for a fisherman, coming in from Alberoni, declared that he had seen the death-ship upon the lagoon and that the destruction of the city was at hand.

" I saw it, signori ; I heard the death-bell ringing. A man lay upon the ship with a dagger in his heart. Before the Cross I swear it. He who rowed the boat was not of this world. There were devils to set the sails of it ; there was the fire of hell at the prow. Let the city hearken, for it is the warning of God."

The tale was told to the Council and to the police on the eve of the great feast. It spread through the city as the news of a mighty disaster. No child in Venice was so young that he had not heard his mother tell the story of the death-ship; the story of that phantom gondola, which spirits rowed upon the lagoons of Venice to warn the city of some misfortune about to visit her, to tell of sickness, perchance, and of the harvesting of death.

Even strong men quailed at the news of it. Women held their children in their arms and hurried to the churches; the priests proclaimed the judgment of God and denounced the sins of the people. But the omen of death was everywhere. And anon a new terror came swiftly upon the trembling city. For an unknown hand set red crosses upon the houses of the doomed, and where the hand wrote, there a man died before the sun dawned again.

The fisherman told his tale, and Venice listened greedily. From that moment all thought of masquerade and carnival ceased. The bells of the churches rang no more; there were no lights in the cafés on the great square; the booths of the clowns were shut, and the zanni starved within them. Even the educated, who laughed at the fisherman's story, laughed no more when every morning brought some new account of assassination and of fatality.

" A fool's tale," they said ; "and yet we see men die. Some enemy of Venice, surely, has come back to reckon with her. She has dealt roughly with the best of her soldiers since the monk Giovanni ruled us. Sforza, lord of Milan ; Andrea Foscari, the swordsman ; Christoforo, Count of Carmagnola, — such men, when they are banished, do not sleep in the mountains. Let the police get news of them, and they will know why the red cross is on the houses."

But the poor, grown old in their superstitions, would listen to no words of reason.

" The death-ship is on the sea! " they cried. " We have looked upon it with our own eyes. Those who have died are but grains of the harvest which must fall. Woe to Venice, for this is the Day of Judgment!"

II

THE Feast of the Ascension passed, and all day long a crowd of the terrified people gazed seawards over the still lagoon, as though it might see with its own eyes the phantom ship, which had come out of the unknown to warn the city.

In the booth of old Barbarino, the first of the clowns of Venice, gloomy faces and heavy sighs marked the close of those black hours. Little Nina herself, — Nina the dancing-girl, who had been called the Daughter of Venice, — no one listened to her when she laughed at the people's stories.

"Who can call back the sun?" exclaimed old Barbarino, wearily, as the seemingly interminable day at length drew to its close; "every morning a body in the water, every night the death-ship on the lagoon. Shall we create the stars, my daughter, as Joshua in the Scriptures? Do your nuns teach you that?"

Nina, the child of the people, clung lovingly to her superstitions; but the education, which Venice had given her at the convent of the Cistercian nuns, had done not a little to moderate them.

"Your death-ship is a cloud upon the water," she said quietly; "if the people are frightened to-day, they will laugh to-morrow. He who sets the red crosses upon the houses will go presently to the columns of the Piazzetta, and there will be a rope for his neck. Frà Giovanni is in Rome, or we should have come to our senses before this day. But they say that the Ascension brings him back, and then — "

She spoke as a little prophetess, for her faith in the great monk, Giovanni, the ruler of Venice, was unshaken. She had won his friendship for herself and for the clowns who flocked to her father's booth. In her eyes Frà Giovanni was all-powerful to work miracles, even to raise the very dead. Had he been in Venice, she argued, a word from him would have quieted the people's folly and brought them back to reason. But old Barbarino, who had never loved the priests, was to be put off with no such tale.

" Let your monk make us bread from the stones and I will believe in him," he retorted. " If he is the people's friend, as he says, why does he permit the people to die? Believe it not, little Nina. We shall be on the road to Florence before the week is out, and God help us as we go."

She would not argue with him, but quitted that melancholy home of hers, and set out to wander, she knew not whither. It was the first hour of evening then; no gondolas were to be seen on the canals at such an hour. The cafés, the shops, the theatres were all deserted. In the churches the music of

vespers for the dead made a dirge of the
night. Men, masked and with their cloaks
muffled about their faces, went hurriedly to
their homes. The hand of the unknown
assassin might be raised for them at any
corner. Panic drove them to their houses.
A young priest, standing at the door of the
church of Santa Maria della Salute, recognised the little dancing-girl as she put off
her boat from the quay, and bade her begone.

"It is for such as you that Venice is to
perish," he said harshly.

Nina did not answer him. She was accustomed to the contempt of the priests. The
love of Venice and the friendship of the
master of Venice were her recompense. And
now, as she sought her consolation, she was
recalled to a memory of this friend by the
voice of one of the people's prophets, who
cried from the bridge of Rialto, —

"Woe to Venice, for the red cross is on
the house of Giovanni, the priest, and to-
morrow he must die."

III

THE dancing-girl heard the words, clear and distinct above the murmur of voices and the rippling water. They were repeated again and again as the prophet turned towards the narrow streets of the Merceria. She heard them echoing afar as a low murmur of sound, and still she sat terrified and motionless.

"The red cross is on the house of Giovanni, the priest, and to-morrow he must die."

Until this time she had paid little heed to the stories of assassination and of death, of which the whole city was full. Perchance she did not credit them, or set them down to the terror of the women and the ignorance of the people. But now the truth of them came to her in an instant. Frà Giovanni — the great priest who had been her friend when she was friendless, — the benefactor who had saved her father from his follies a hundred times — would the unknown assassin strike even at him? The thought brought the blood to her cheeks. From the first moment when she heard the prophet crying, it came to her that God had sent her to the bridge that she might hear the words and help her friend.

She had left her father's booth in the little boat the clowns used upon the lagoon. The house of the Capuchin monk stood upon the island known as the Guidecca, the island of the Jews. To reach it she must cross the great expanse of water before the Piazzetta; that lagoon whereon the apparition had been seen; that lagoon which no boatman of Venice would now face after nightfall, even though one had offered him a thousand ducats for the ferry.

Fear of it appalled her; yet courage drove her on. She would dare all for her friend's sake. To warn Frà Giovanni, — to warn her friend, who had been in Rome and might know nothing of the red cross or its meaning! She braved all else in that consuming desire.

Her boat touched the quay of the priest's house just as darkness came down upon the city. A lantern at the gate of it showed her the red cross painted boldly upon the postern. She was still debating how she should tell Frà Giovanni her news when she saw the monk himself pacing the garden and coming towards her. He, in turn, had heard the splash of oars; and when he observed the little boat and the face of her who rowed it, a cry of wonder escaped him.

" Thou, child — and alone ! "

She did not know how to answer him. The keen black eyes of the monk seemed to read her very heart. She could not tell him why she had come to the house. There was nothing hidden from the mind of Frà Giovanni, she thought. And he must have laughed at her already.

" I heard them crying strange things at Rialto," she stammered; "they said that you had come back from Rome and that the red cross was upon the house. I could not hear such things, Excellency; I came to tell you of them."

She laughed at herself afterwards because she had called him " Excellency," but he was asking himself what courage was that which had carried the dancing-girl where no boatman dared to pass.

" You càme alone, Nina ; did you not fear the people's stories ? " he asked.

She shrugged her shoulders.

" The things we fear need not be true," she said. " I heard the stories, — how that men die every day in Venice, and that the death-ship is on the waters. But who will trouble about a dancing-girl ? Men do not strike at the poor while there are the rich of the city to think about. It is of you I would speak, father. There was no hope while you were in Rome, but now, you will save the city from its follies, you will give the people bread again?"

She stood pleading before him. He remembered another day three years ago, when, on that very spot, she had told him of the conspiracy in the church of the Servites, and had begged of him the life of the man she loved, Christoforo, the banished Count of Carmagnola. He said to himself that in all Italy there was not one with the courage and the heart of this little dancing-girl.

"Nina," he said very gently, "was it that I might save your father's house again that you came here to-night?"

She was silent at the question. He read her answer in that silence, and took both her hands in his.

"Not so," he said; "I know your story, little one. Go now to your home again. Three years ago you saved Venice from her enemies. Who knows that you may not save her once more this night? Go back across the waters, then, and fear nothing, whatever sights you see. And if men question you — as assuredly they will — bid them look upon the waters, where they shall find the answer of Venice and of Giovanni the monk."

He led her to the *riva* of the house, and watched her boat earnestly as she rowed it towards the darkness of the lagoon.

" They will follow her," he muttered to himself; " they will follow her."

Swiftly turning, he called a servant to him. " Let the police know that we have need of them," he said. " The clown's daughter will show us to-night the house of the assassins."

IV

THOUGH it was a night of May, and there had been a great heat of the sun all day, heavy mists steamed up from the waters of the lagoon; and so black was the hour that little Nina in her boat soon lost sight of the welcome lights upon the island, and could discern no lanterns upon the Piazza or even in the houses by the nearer church of Santa Maria della Salute. While she was talking to the priest, all memory of her fears had left her; but now that she rowed alone upon the broad of the channel an apprehension, as great as any she had ever known, came back to trouble her, and to set her hands trembling upon the oars.

These tales the people told; how if there should be truth in them! She remembered the story of the fisherman, who swore before the Cross that he had seen the death-ship of the fables — that phantom gondola which the dead rowed and the spirits of the dead haunted. She said she would believe in no tale so foolish, and, so saying, began to believe in it the more.

It was very dark upon the lagoon, and strangely silent. Sometimes sturdy strokes shot her boat swiftly towards the distant Piazzetta. Or, again, she would drift with the sleepy current, and listen for the voices of her imagination. Always she remembered the strange words of the priest: "Who knows that you may not save Venice this night!" Whatever befell, Frà Giovanni would protect her, she thought.

Yet how could she, Nina, the daughter of Barbarino the clown, save Venice? Once before, in the church of the Servites, she had lived through a night of terror, and had discovered those who would have betrayed the city. She had delivered up to justice the man whom, in her folly, she had chosen to love. But such a night would never return. She said that she was alone on the waters, and that God looked down upon her. She did not know that the enemies of Venice were watching her as she rowed. "A spy," they said, and were determined already upon her punishment.

The remembrance that none would trouble about a dancing-girl gave her heart, and carried her a little way further toward her home. When she ceased to row for the second time, a sound as of a muffled oar beating the waters struck suddenly upon her ears, and held her wondering. She was sure that she heard the sound; sure that it was quite near her. Yet when she peered into the darkness she saw nothing but the quaint figures of the mist, the little waves, and the black water of the stream. It would be some venturesome traveller who knew nothing of the people's stories, she said. A sense of loneliness and of danger approaching was not to be resisted. If the people had not lied! If there should be strange sights upon the lagoon!

She rowed again a little way; again she

let her boat drift upon the stream. But this time no surmise, no sound of muffled oars held her still. In all her life she had never known so great a premonition of danger. For a strange light fell suddenly upon her face; it came she knew not whence. The surrounding water shone as silver beneath its rays; she saw the light as a bright phosphorescent glow upon her boat, upon her hands. Everything about her was enveloped in it. She sat spellbound with the rays of that unearthly lantern turned full upon her.

The light shone out and darkness succeeded to it. She heard the sound of muffled oars no more; only the surging of the waves as they beat against the prow of a ship. And she became conscious of some presence; a presence which was not of things known but of the mysteries unnameable. The fisherman had told a true tale, after all, then! Dread of something beyond the knowledge of men appalled her. She feared to see the death-ship; and, fearing, her eyes beheld it.

Again the white light shone upon the waters. The fount of it hung as a ball of fire above the still lagoon. In the aureole of the light, she beheld a long, black gondola;

and he who rowed it had the face as of the devils in the pictures of the painters. Prone in the cabin of the boat, where candles burned and windows of glass permitted all the world to wonder at the sight, there lay the body of a man with a veil thrown across his face. She perceived that the man did not move and that his limbs were rigid; she knew that Venice would hear again to-morrow of the death of one of her sons.

At the bow of the gondola there stood a strange figure, as of a man masked in a beast's head, with horns and large ears, and a sword in his hand. A flame of red fire, burning at his feet, cast a crimson glow upon the shining blade and the strange disguise. Nina had never seen, even in the fantasies of the painters, a spectacle so terrible. She did not cry out; she did not try to speak to the man; no fear of things human withered her courage. She thought that she had seen a vision from the world beyond the grave; from that world of which the priests had spoken to terrify the people and bring them to repentance.

A vision, indeed, yet one very near to her eyes now. She could distinguish the ring upon the finger of the dead man who lay in the cabin; she could see the mirror of the great lantern which diffused the phosphorescent light. He who held the sword, and was masked in the beast's head, gave an order to the steersman, and turned towards her. She did not raise her voice nor move from her seat. All things happened as in some moment of her sleep.

She saw the shadow of the great boat magnified and approaching; she beheld more clearly the visage of him who stood at the bow; she felt strong arms winding about her body as the man stooped and lifted her to the deck of the gondola. The end had come, she thought — and neither speaking to them nor wrestling with the hand that held her, she fainted in the arms of the unknown, and the ship and lights vanished from her sight.

V

NINA recovered consciousness in a vast room, like to no room she had ever seen. They had laid her on a couch of silk; and in her waking moments she believed that she was in her father's booth again, and that all she had suffered had been the terror of a dream. But when she opened her eyes, she beheld a roof painted by one of the great artists of Venice; and from the ceiling a great chandelier of glass depending; and in the chandelier many candles brightly burning.

Anon, she turned her eyes towards the centre of the room, and perceived there a table shining with an abundance of silver, and half hidden by fruit and flowers and the long red flasks for the wine. None but a noble of the city could sit at such a table, she thought. Nor could she so much as imagine how she came to such a place, or why she lay, with limbs benumbed and a strange sense of physical weakness, alone in that great room.

There had been no one near her when first she opened her eyes; but while she was still trying to gather up the threads of her own strange story, she distinguished the voices of people in an antechamber, and presently someone uttered the name of Frà Giovanni, and she heard men laughing at it. After a little while the laughter ceased, and a voice exclaimed:

"If it lie between the priest and Francesco, there will be a monk the less at dawn."

Nina heard the voice, and understood it. Her wits were ever quick; and out of the story of the night they were shaping the truth for her. The phantom gondola — those that rowed it were but men, after all, then! The banished enemies of Venice must be its masters, employing it to terrify the people, and to cloak their own crimes. There was no other mystery but the mystery of vengeance awakened. Those who had set the red cross upon the house of the father of Venice were those in whose power she was.

"If it lie between the priest and Francesco — !"

She repeated the words, and began to find the meaning of them. She said that while she was a prisoner in that unknown house the assassin had gone already to the island of the Jews. When the sun rose, the man who had bestowed so great a friendship upon her, the man whom Venice loved as never she had loved citizen before, would be no more. Her own helplessness seemed pitiful to her as she confessed the truth. If she had been a man! There were tears in her eyes when she remembered that a brave man might have saved her friend.

It was a splendid apartment in which she now found herself — a room in one of the greatest of the palaces, she thought. She could see immense painted doors, which shut it off from the antechamber; one of these doors was half-open, and she distinguished, beyond it, the glitter of the gold on the doublet of a man, and the hilt of a sword studded with diamonds. There had been no time to think of herself as yet; but when she saw the man she became conscious of her peril; and with a step trained to lightness from her childhood, she darted across the room towards the long windows of the balcony.

If she could but open those windows, and cry out to any gondolier who might pass the house! When she drew back the curtains, the folly of her plan disclosed itself, for the window was boarded over, and bands of iron drew the boards together so that no ray of light could pass the chinks.

She drew back from the window as from the bars of a prison. The splendour of the room had put out of her head until this moment the memory of the circumstances under which she had come to the house. But now she realised them fully. The enemies of Venice had known of her visit, and had trapped her. There could be no hope that she might ever leave that room again to go and tell of all the things she had seen and the voices she had heard. The men would kill her to save themselves. She had looked upon the sun and the water for the last time.

She was but a child still in mind, if not in years, and the fear of death was very terrible to her. Gifted with an imagination above the common, she foresaw the moment when she would lie, still and voiceless, upon the floor of the room. There could be no hope of mercy in that place. She heard her heart beating as she crept from the window; she feared even the velvet tread of her little feet.

A man entered the room and stood to watch her curiously. He was a young man, and he wore a suit of black velvet, slashed with gold. She met his gaze face to face, and recognised him as Andrea Foscari, a noble whom Venice had banished three years before that day. There was no look of anger on his face, for the beauty of the dancing-girl, as she stood in the aureole of light, fascinated him.

"Well," he said, "so our little prisoner is awake again."

"My lord," she asked pitifully, "why have you brought me to this house?"

"I have brought you to sup, little Nina. The spirits were hungry, and would not wait."

He spoke banteringly, and turned to call his companions.

"Gian," he said, "here is the little spy waiting for her supper. She is going to tell us why she went to the Guidecca to-night. Let Benedetto bring the guitar, and she will dance for us — eh, my Nina, you will show us afterwards how you dance upon the Piazzetta?"

He came nearer to her and clasped her hand. She drew back from him, for his fingers were hot and burning and she knew that he was lying to her.

"Tell me," he asked in a low voice, "what carried you to the Guidecca to-night?"

"My lord," she answered vaguely, "I must go back to my home. My father is waiting for me!"

He laughed ironically.

"Oh," he said, "the clown weeps for his daughter; clown's tears, little Nina, which we will go to see to-morrow — when you have earned your liberty."

Other men came into the room to the number of four, men in robes of violet and white, with jewels sparkling at their throats and in the hilts of their daggers. One of them, who seemed to be their leader, a man with the fair hair of a Saxon, came towards the girl and clutched her arm savagely.

"Child," he said, "why were you upon the lagoon to-night?"

"My lord," she exclaimed, still thinking of her home, "let me go to my father's house and I will tell no one — "

He stamped his foot angrily.

"Answer me," he said, "or they shall find your body in the water. What brought you upon the lagoon to-night?"

She looked up at him and answered unflinchingly:

"I went to warn Giovanni, the priest."

An oath rose to the man's lips. He half unsheathed his dagger. She thought that he was about to strike her down; but, as he stood irresolute, someone entered the room, and all eyes were turned towards the door.

"Christoforo — you here!"

Nina heard the name, but did not dare to raise her eyes.

Christoforo, the lord of Carmagnola, the man who had been a leader of Venice three years before that day, the man whose life she had saved in the church of the Servites — was he, then, among the assassins?

The Count entered the room quickly. He looked at the girl and at the men who surrounded her. There was a flush of blood to his cheeks when he saw the half-sheathed dagger; and he did not need to ask the intention of him who held it.

"Great God!" he cried. "Have you brought me from the mountains for this?"

The man's hand dropped to his side. He answered mockingly.

"Ha!" he said, "here is our patron, then. But you come to Venice too late, Count. The work is done. Francesco is already at the priest's house. This child followed us on the lagoon to-night, and we brought her here. Release her, and she will carry our story to the police. You will share our bed, and we have not made it with feathers."

Carmagnola heard him contemptuously.

"You were born to the bravo's cloak, Galeazzo," he said scornfully; "by all accounts you have worn that cloak well in Venice. Come, let me see this tale-bearer."

He pushed the man roughly aside, and crossed to the girl's side.

"Who are you, child?" he asked in a gentle voice.

She raised her head and looked at him. A great cry of recognition escaped his lips. He had last seen Nina of Venice in the church of the Servites, and she had saved his life there.

"Thou!" he said, "here in the Palazzo Andrea?"

"It is I, Lord Count," she answered simply.

He raised her in his arms. The others stood dumb; they knew that they were face to face with one of the greatest swordsmen in Italy.

"Little Nina," he asked, "what brought you to this house?"

She did not know why she answered him as she did, or how it was that the priest's words came to her in that instant. Another's will commanded her to speak, and she said very quietly:

"Lord Count, if you will look upon the water, you will see my answer."

Carmagnola regarded her perplexedly. Silence, the silence of curiosity, was upon the others. Foscari, himself, ran to the window, and opening a panel in the boards looked out at the black canal below. When he had stood there an instant he turned to the others, and they saw the whiteness of his face.

"Well?" they asked.

"The ship is there, and a body is on the bier," he replied. "It is the body of Francesco."

A savage cry of rage burst from the lips of Galeazzo as he and the three remaining ran to the window. They thought that they had heard a lie, but when they looked out they saw their own death-ship; and upon it there lay the body of the assassin Francesco, who had been sent to the house of Giovanni, the priest. A dagger was still in the man's heart; his head lay over the gunwale of the boat, and the water lapped upon his streaming hair.

"Well," asked Carmagnola, "and what do you see, signori?"

"The work of the spy whose hand you hold!" exclaimed Galeazzo, fiercely. "Yonder lies Francesco, dead. Would you send the child back now, signore?"

He did not wait for any answer, but drew his dagger, and stood anew to the attack. For an instant Nina heard the cries of the four; she beheld the blades flashing as points of silver in the light; she saw the figure of the lord of Carmagnola as he drew his sword and beat the daggers down. Then, as in some hour of miracle, the great doors of the room were burst open, and she knew that the Guards of Venice were the masters of the house.

"Signori," said the Captain of the Guard, ironically, "they wait for you at the Palace."

No one answered him. They knew that he had spoken a sentence of death.

VI

VERY early on the following morning the story of Nina of Venice was known throughout the city. Frà Giovanni told it, and added ornament to it. She, the dancing-girl, had crossed the lagoon, that lagoon where no boatman of Venice would have ventured after sunset for an oar of gold; she had crossed it to save the priest whom Venice loved. The police had followed her as she went. Unknowingly she had been the link between them and the house of the assassins. They had seen her dragged from her boat; had followed the phantom gondola and learnt at last that the Palazzo Andrea sheltered the enemies of Venice.

Day had scarcely dawned when a mighty concourse of the people gathered before the booth of Barbarino, the clown, and proclaimed with frenzied cries that the night of mystery was no more.

"She has shown to Venice the house of the assassin. *Viva*, Nina, the dancer. *Viva*, our daughter! There was no death-ship, after all, comrades. It lies yonder at the *riva* of the Palace. Long life to our Father Giovanni."

Nina heard the cries, yet showed her face to none. She had not slept through those hours of excitement and of fear. She remembered one who then lay in the dungeons of the Palace. He might even then be dead. She cared nothing for the people's favour or the rewards of which they spoke. She loved a man to whom she had spoken but twice in her life. When the sun set she knew that her lover would have ceased to live.

" They will punish the innocent with the guilty," she thought. " There will be none to believe it. No one will listen to Nina, the dancing-girl."

So she reasoned as the day broke, and all the world of Venice flocked to the great Piazza. Terror dominated the city no more. Death no longer stalked the dark places. Fathers would not weep for sons to-morrow, nor mistresses for their lovers. What the Signori of the Night had been unable to do, this waif of the booths had done. She had saved Venice from her follies, and the city would remember.

There had been a meeting of the Council of Three at six o'clock that morning; but it was noon before the Guards of the Palace came to the booth on the Piazzetta and asked for the clown's daughter.

" The Signori await her in the Council Chamber," the Captain said. " Let her fear nothing, for all is known."

The people heard the words and came anew to the door of the booth. Above the clamour of their voices, the music of bells and the blare of trumpets prevailed. No procession which Carnival had given to Venice surpassed that procession to the Palace. Women wept; children cast flowers in the path the Guards must tread. But Nina saw neither the flowers nor the people. The face of the man she loved was ever before her. She had heard again the words he had spoken to her yesterday.

Within the Palace there were many of the nobles of the city, of her priests and her rich men. A great crowd thronged the staircase leading to the Sala dei Capi where the Three sat. Nina distinguished no faces, heard none of the compliments addressed to her. She remembered afterwards that she stood as one in a dream while the President of the Three spoke to her. But there were few of his words which she could repeat, and it was not until the end of his address that she began to listen to it.

"The city will reward you, in some part at our dictation, in some part as you yourself shall choose. The Palazzo Andrea, forfeit to the State by reason of the crimes you have discovered, will be held in perpetuity by you and the children that shall be born to you.

Beyond this, Venice gives you the life of one of the six prisoners you brought to justice last night. In that choice she seeks nothing but your own will and pleasure; she imposes no conditions. He whom you name will to-day be sent to the Palazzo Andrea, where his place of captivity must be."

A smile of amusement passed over the faces of those in the room. Nina did not understand it. One of the officers, who was at her side, whispered: "Answer the Lord President, child."

She stared at him, and said nothing.

"Well," continued the President, "and the name of the prisoner to whom the Serene Prince is willing to grant this conditional pardon?"

"My lord," she said, "I do not understand, I do not hear——"

He took her hand encouragingly.

"Child," he said, "Venice gives you the life and the custody of one of those condemned by her to death this day. There are the prisoners. Name one of them to us, and he is this moment free."

He made a signal to the guard, and those who last night had supped in the Palazzo

Andrea were brought into the room. An overwhelming consciousness of happiness came suddenly to the trembling dancing-girl. She fell at the feet of Christoforo, the Count of Carmagnola.

"My lords," she said, "I have chosen."